paythepiper

∽ FORTHCOMING FROM STARSCAPE ∽

Troll Bridge: A Rock 'n' Roll Fairy Tale
Jane Yolen and Adam Stemple

paythepiper

A ROCK 'N' ROLL FAIRY TALE

JANE YOLEN AND ADAM STEMPLE

STARSCAPE

A TOM DOHERTY ASSOCIATES BOOK
NEW YORK

PAY THE PIPER: A ROCK 'N' ROLL FAIRY TALE

Copyright © 2005 by Jane Yolen and Adam Stemple

This book is printed on acid-free paper.

A Starscape Book
Published by Tom Doherty Associates, LLC
175 Fifth Avenue
New York, NY 10010

www.starscapebooks.com

Library of Congress Cataloging-in Publication Data

Yolen, Jane.
    Pay the piper / Jane Yolen and Adam Stemple.—1st ed.
        p. cm.— (A rock 'n' roll tale)
    "A Tom Doherty Associates book."
    Summary: When Callie interviews the band Brass Rat for her school newspaper, her feelings
are ambivalent, but when all the children of Northampton begin to disappear on Halloween,
she knows where the dangerous search must begin.
    ISBN 0-765-31158-5 (acid-free paper)
    EAN 978-0765-31158-0
    [1. Missing children—Fiction.   2. Rock music—Fiction.   3. Bands (Music)—Fiction.
    4. Magic—Fiction.   5. Space and time—Fiction.   6. Fantasy.] I. Stemple, Adam.
    II. Title.

PZ7.Y78Pay 2005
[Fic}—dc22

                                                                        2004060118

First Edition: July 2005

Printed in the United States of America

0   9   8   7   6   5   4   3   2   1

For big David, forever
—J. Y.

For Alison and wee David,
fey children I am proud to call my own
—A. S.

∽

With special thanks to Greg Feeley.

And apologies to Northampton and Hadley, Massachusetts, for any liberties we have taken with their geographies, as well as apologies to Smith College, whose John M. Greene Hall was pressed into service for the Brass Rat concert, though it really only holds about half of the audience we proposed for it.

∾ Contents ∾

∾ From the Authors ∾

Based on a true event, the tale of the Pied Piper of Hamelin (or as they spelled it in German, Hameln) has always fascinated us. We are both musicians and storytellers and the piper was a performer so talented he didn't just entertain his audience—he enchanted them!

This is what is known about the reputed piper: On the 26th of June, 1284, "came a colorful piper to Hamelin and led 130 children away . . ." At least this is what the earliest account—a piece of Latin prose—says some 150 years after the event.

More interesting than the bare fact is the *why* of it.

Why did the piper come and why did the children leave with him? Some scholars say that they went off on a crusade, or that they were recruited as settlers for Northern Germany or Transylvania. Some say the town had the Black Plague and the children had to be led out of town to save them. Some guess that the children had eaten bread infected with ergot, a disease of rye grain that leads to bizarre dancing and shaking. Some people have even theorized that the Pied Piper was an alien and that the children were swept off of earth in a UFO.

The legend of the Pied Piper is now a tourist gimmick in the (very real) town of Hameln. Poets like Robert Browning and Goethe have written about the piper. Operas, musicals, pantomimes, and ballets based on the story have been produced. Children's books telling the story in dozens of languages have been published. Pop groups like Jethro Tull and Abba have written songs based on it. And scholarly papers by the dozens have been penned trying to explain just what really happened so long ago in that small town.

Being novelists, we have come up with a different idea altogether, one that has little to do with Hamelin and a lot to do with Faerie. If it is an unlikely explanation, at least it fits all the known facts. And clears up a few other mysterious disappearances that history has left unexplained.

Because *what if* the events in Hamelin had been just a small piece of a very big pie? That was our starting point. The answer becomes then: Could we in our very modern clothes actually—someday—be forced to Pay the Piper?

—Jane Yolen and Adam Stemple

∞

Come away, O human child!
To the waters and the wild
With a faery, hand in hand,
For the world's more full of weeping
Than you can understand.

—William Butler Yeats

1 - River of Blood

The piper caught sight of the river long before the sound of rushing water reached his ears or the salt smell of blood struck his nose. The river coiled around the landscape like a red serpent below him.

"All the blude that's shed on earth runs thro the springs o' that countrie," his traveling companion intoned, his long face without guile.

The piper grunted but made no other reply. He knew the old song as well as his friend did. Perhaps better.

"One last border to cross," he said. One last border, *he meant, and his exile would begin in earnest.*

What a strange word *exile* is, *he thought.* To be x-ed out, sent away from one's home, that place of serenity and peace. Never to live again at home, the country of the Ever Fair, where death has such small dominion.

Picking his way along the bonny road toward the final border, he realized that his father was not going to forgive him. Somewhere, deep down, he had always believed his punishment a sham, had always believed that his father would be following them at a distance, waiting for the right moment to call them back and say that all was forgiven.

Forgiven or forgotten. That it was all a misunderstanding. That his brother, the heir, had recovered from what had seemed a fatal blow.

But his father's curse, once spoken, had been binding. No one followed behind. And the blow his brother had suffered had certainly been fatal, as the piper well knew.

After all, he was the one who had dealt it.

2 · Family Jokes

Getting ready for school, Callie looked into the mirror, tugging at her pumpkin-colored hair with an old brush. She wished she could blame either her mother or father for the color, but they were both dishwater blondes. No one in the family on either side—so her mother had assured her—had ever had hair that color before.

"The milkman," Dad often quipped, winking and then laughing uproariously. Callie had been ten before she got it, the year they taught biology in her elementary school. She'd come home, slammed her books onto the kitchen table, and shouted, "No more heredity jokes." Only she'd said "hera-dairy" instead, which had become a family joke in itself.

Family jokes.

"This whole family is a joke," Callie said. She exaggerated her voice so that she sounded like Morticia on the *Addams Family*, but deep inside she knew that she meant it.

First, there was the question of her name. Calcephony. It was a leftover from her parents' romance with the 60s, though they'd hardly been alive then. She knew it could have been worse. They'd talked about Evenstar and Dawn Rider and even Turalura before settling on Calcephony.

Of course, when she'd first taken violin lessons, they'd laughed and said they should have named her Cacophony because that's what the violin sounded like. *Cacophony*—which meant an awful noise, as any competent dictionary would say.

Her friends just called her Callie, and that suited her much better.

Callie stuck her tongue out at the mirror. The tongue was white-coated, as if she'd some wasting disease. Not that she'd tell her parents. They'd make her stay home and dose her with herbal medications that tasted as if they still had dirt on the roots. She didn't mind skipping school when she was sick. She wasn't some grade wonk after all. But it would mean staying home from the evening concert, too. And after all she'd done to convince her parents to let her go.

Well, at least to let the *family* go. Her mom and her dad and her tagalong brother Nick. For Nickelodeon. Much worse than Calcephony, even she had to admit.

And even harder to take was her older brother's name—Marsepolus. He was in his last year in college, and probably delighted to be far away. Now he was known as Mars. But what he'd had to go through—Mars Bars, Martian, Marsupial, Marzipan. It was astonishing he was so even-tempered.

Honestly, Callie thought, *parents should be trained before they are allowed to name their children. Trained with a whip, like any wild animals.*

THE WHOLE CONCERT THING HAD started on a Monday two weeks earlier. Callie had heard through the school grapevine that a really hot band was coming to the Valley.

"Faster than a speeding ticket," was how her best friend Josee always described the school rumor-mill. Josee had a way with words. Lots of words.

"Which band?" Callie asked.

"Brass Rat!" Josee actually squealed the name, then twisted a piece of her black hair. Josee had hair like mattress springs, dark, oiled, coiled. She was long-legged, like a colt. "Brass Rat is the single most, industrial-strength, ever-bopping, high-flying, celestial . . ." That was Josee. Never one word where a dozen could do.

Now even Callie had heard of Brass Rat—who hadn't? But they weren't on her Top Ten, or even her Top Twenty, though maybe the next five after that. A folk rock band— "rock and reel" Josee called them—when what Callie really preferred was either straight folk or straight rock.

"Coming here? To the Valley? You have *got* to be kidding!" She was really stunned. No bands ever came to the Valley that she'd heard of. Well, almost no one. Certainly no one on her Top Ten—or even Top Twenty.

Josee had nodded and opened her mouth to speak. But Alison—who always seemed attached to Josee at the hip and was therefore Callie's second best friend by default— squealed. "Next Friday squared!" If Josee used lots of words, Alison spoke in shorthand. And as tall as Josee was, Alison was short and round, with strange long arms, which made her look like she'd been drawn by a three-year-old. But she made up in heart what she lacked in words or height.

Callie knew that "Next Friday squared" meant two weeks from that Friday. On the day before Halloween.

"I'm going to work on my folks, two-prong attack, back and front, a regular army up-and-at-'em, they'll never know what hit them," said Josee.

Callie guessed that getting to the concert was going to be a piece of cake for Josee. Her parents hardly kept an eye on her. Or an ear. She was a latchkey kid supreme.

"Me two," squealed Alison.

"Me three." Callie had said it without much enthusiasm. She hardly expected her parents to give her permission. For all their joking, and their bad taste in names, her parents were really quite strict. When talking to her friends, Callie called them the Parent Trap, meaning they kept her entrapped, tailed, jailed, and nailed. She had to sign in and sign out whenever she went anywhere. She'd even been fingerprinted and registered with the local police from the time she was one. Maybe *that* was understandable. Mars had gone missing one evening when he was seven, doing a walkabout. Gone up into a neighbor's tree house to spend the night on his own. It had scared them all silly. Especially Mars, because an owl roosting in the next tree had cried out like a baby half the night. Mars had been too scared to scream for help, or to come down on his own. The police had found him in the morning. After that, they were all fingerprinted and the doors had been triple locked from the inside and there was an alarm system that Callie was sure rivaled the National Mint's.

No, Callie hardly expected permission from her parents to go to a concert on her own, but a plan had begun to form that very moment. Callie was good with plans. With *her* parents, she had to be.

"I'll tell them I'm writing a story about the band for the school paper," she told her friends. "Schoolwork trumps everything in their universe."

"Phantasmagoric!" said Josee. "Supercal and all that."

"Double," Alison added.

A moment's worry hit Callie. "Do you think they'll go for it?"

"It'll work like a charm, like a magic spell, like . . ." Josee began.

"Clockwork," Alison finished for her.

Callie smiled at them. They were not only her best friends, they were her cheering section. "Thanks."

THAT AFTERNOON, WITH A NOTE from her journalism teacher, and a number to call at the concert venue, Callie went home to put her plan into action.

Her parents had surprised her. Callie was still amazed at how easily they'd been convinced. It'd been a piece of cake. An enormous slice, actually.

"Brass Rat?" her dad had said, running fingers through his thinning blonde hair. He'd looked down at the flier Callie thrust at him. Dog-eared and messy with fingerprints, it had been downloaded off the Internet, then passed around at school to those few friends who didn't have e-mail. "I love them. We saw them back when Mars was an infant and . . ."

Yada, yada, yada, Callie had thought, not listening. *In the good old rock-and-roll days. In the Cretaceous.* Of course she doubted that was possible. The band members were all young and hot. But she was careful not to say this aloud. Instead, fluttering her eyelids, she looked up at her dad with what passed for quiet adoration. "Then . . ." and let the question hang in the air.

He took the bait. "Maybe . . ."

That's when she'd set the hook deep. "The family never goes to things *together* anymore. Not since Mars went off to college."

He'd turned. "Myrna," he called to her mom. "Listen up. I've got a great idea."

And then, just to totally embarrass Callie, he began to sing one of the early Brass Rat songs.

"Under the hill, under the stone,
No one can touch me, for I am alone,
No one can reach me, no one can dare,
No one can love me, and I do not care."

"Harmony!" her mom shouted as she came into the room, her voice warbling about a half an octave above his.

Oh God, no! Callie thought, her parents were fans! She was thankful her friends weren't around to hear them.

Except for the plan, Callie would have run out of the room, slamming the door behind her. But she stayed. Stayed and said with sweet conviction when they were finished, "Gee—I didn't know you knew Brass Rat that well."

"We know that one song," Mom said. "It was a number one back when Mars was a toddler. Got to hear them somewhere, I forget where. Didn't know they were still together. Dan—we have to go to the concert! The whole family."

The whole family? Callie's stomach flopped over. "But Mars is at school."

"Well, we'll see if he wants to come home for the weekend," her mother amended.

Her father shook his head. "Halloween's big at his school. Costume parties and . . ."

Breaking into song again, her mother sang the next two lines:

"I do not care, for I am a stone,
No one can touch me, for I am alone."

Then she laughed. "What a sad-sack song that is. I wonder what his problem was."

"No wifey, no kidlets." Her father reached out a hand.

In a minute it was going to get seriously icky. Callie decided intervention was her only hope. "So who will come?"

They were holding hands now, but at least they'd stopped singing and talking baby talk. "Your mom, me, you—and Nick," her father said.

In order to throw them off the scent, she said with a deep frown, "Does Nick have to come, too?" Though Nick would keep the two of them busy.

"If you want to go, Nick goes, too," her dad said. "And you'll take him to the interview as well."

That was *definitely* not part of her plan. This time her frown was real.

"Dad . . ." she wailed.

But there was to be no winning this argument. Callie left the room and slammed the door.

3 · Talent

A cold thin drizzle wormed its way down the window. The piper sighed. He could smoke his one cigarillo under the canopy, but it wouldn't be pleasant.

The trouble with habits, *he thought,* was not that they could kill you. It was that they could be boring for an eternity. *He turned up the collar of his pea coat and went out into the wet and the cold.*

A family with two kids, a thin girl with orange ragweed hair about fourteen, a boy about seven with wide speedwell eyes, went past him, running into the warmth of the hall. So intent were they to get in out of the rain, they didn't recognize him.

Fame is fleeting, *his mother had always told him.* Family is forever.

"And alliteration is annoying," he had replied once, lashing out and trying to hurt her feelings. He was brash and bitter then, as all young men are when they begin yearning to make their own mark on the world. And feel the bonds of their family like chains.

But his mother had merely patted his head and whispered in his ear, "You are my favorite, you know. So talented . . ."

The cigarillo suddenly tasted bitter and he spit three times and muttered a curse in the old tongue.

Talented, *he thought.* Not wise like my older brother, nor brave like my younger. But talented.

He ground the cigarillo out on his boot heel.

Time to go in and put that talent to work.

Time to sing for his supper.

Time to rock and roll.

4 · At the Concert

Nick tugged on Callie's press pass which hung around her neck in a plastic pocket. She'd been given it at the door. It had her name in big block letters and her school paper's name underneath, *The Hamper*.

Staring up at her with his little pointy chin lifted, Nick looked like a mini-clone of their father. "Callie, will they be coming out soon?"

They. The band.

Brass Rat.

She hummed a bit of their signature tune, the words running through her brain.

"Out of the darkness and into the light,
We search for a chance to get into the fight. . . ."

She'd spent the last week listening to a couple of her parents' old CDs to soak up what her journalism teacher called *ambiance*. When she'd checked that word in the dictionary, she saw it meant "surroundings." So she had surround-sounded herself with Brass Rat ambiance.

The group itself was about twenty years old, ancient in rock terms. But two of the four members were *much* older than she'd thought. Callie hadn't realized exactly how old until she'd done the research. After checking the printout included in the CDs, she'd gone on to read everything she could find about them on the Internet. Seems Gringras and Alabas had been in bands that had opened for everyone, including the Beatles, the Stones, Aerosmith, and Tina Turner. *Quite a history!*

Given that Gringras and Alabas were apparently rock legends, Callie was stunned that they would come to the Valley and that she was actually at the concert. Along with about five thousand other people.

Minus one, she thought. Her brother Mars. Boy, was he mad he was missing the show! But he was his fraternity's party czar, which meant that he was running their Halloween costume ball and couldn't get away.

Then she thought: *But* I *have a press pass.* That meant she could get up close and personal with the band. Other kids from other schools might have such passes, but Callie knew she was the only reporter from her school who'd wangled one. Probably because she was the only one in journalism class who could actually write. The others were still at the *what's-a-gerund?* stage of grammar.

Nick grabbed her press pass again, being annoying as usual. "When are they gonna get here?" he asked, in his been-in-the-car-too-long whine.

"Any minute, Bugbrain," she told him, then glanced over

at her mother and father who were studiously ignoring the insult. Or else they hadn't heard it. She guessed the latter as they were absolutely wrapped up watching two men dressed all in black who were checking out the instruments onstage.

Suddenly the lights went down.

The crowd began screaming and it was deafening.

Nick grabbed Callie's hand. His palm was icy. "Is it time?"

She was so excited, she didn't let go and instead gave his hand a sisterly squeeze. "Time."

The sold-out hall was dark and loud and, after a minute, she was glad she hadn't let go.

"What's happening?" Nick said. He couldn't see over all the standing, screaming fans.

On tiptoe, Callie tried to make out anything on the stage. The men in black had gone. "Nothing yet." She could feel the tension rising all around her.

A few minutes more, and still Brass Rat hadn't taken the stage. Now there were some catcalls, some scattered murmurings as the crowd began to get restless.

By her side, Nick was turning his head, like the girl in the *Exorcist* movie. Then he dropped her hand and spun around on one leg.

"Nick . . ." she whispered angrily, wondering at the same time if the show was ever going to start.

Then she realized—it already had. A low sound was building, *and it probably had been for some time*. Only now was the sound becoming audible—a note built from the bottom up, finally resolving into a deep, throbbing tone.

Callie glanced behind them, searching for the source of

the sound in the blackened hall, then looked again at the stage. Her eyes had already become accustomed to the darkness, and now she could see things—a bit of movement, a stool, a mike and . . . there!

A small blue spotlight suddenly outlined a lone figure at center stage. He was dressed in what looked like peasant's apparel: a simple cotton shirt, homespun breeches, sturdy leather riding boots. *Unusually tall and thin, but not unattractively so,* she thought. In fact, he looked awfully good for a guy who had to be at least her father's age. Not all wrinkly like Mick Jagger or Paul McCartney.

Yep, she thought, *Peter Gringras is still a hottie, no matter how old he might be.*

Gringras stood in front of the microphone with sinuous fingers wrapped around a silver flute. He appeared to be squeezing that one amazing note out of the instrument. Callie wondered when he would ever take another breath. He began to rock slightly, back and forth, and his clothes—that had first seemed so plain—came alive as if something woven into them caught the light and danced.

He had yet to play a second note and Callie could see that he already owned the crowd. Glancing around—the hall now lit with a warm glow—she made out people swaying to the same rhythm. There was no beat, no meter, just this one long note, yet everyone in the hall seemed to hear the hint of a song, a dance, a celebration.

Gringras began to define it.

What started as one note became two.

Then four.

Then, as the pace and pulses quickened, the notes came

too quick to count. Gringras gyrated madly and his fingers flew across the pads.

The crowd roared as he flipped the flute to the other side and played left-handed. Callie remembered Mrs. Ryder, her fifth grade music teacher, telling her that such a thing was impossible. Yet, there he was, playing left-handed—*sinisterly,* thought Callie, recalling the old word for left—with no discernible drop in skill.

The pitch grew higher and the notes came faster, higher and faster, faster and higher, and Gringras was screaming the notes as he played them until Callie could no longer tell what was voice and what was flute or if it was something else entirely.

Then she knew: At the end, it was his voice. She knew because, as he screamed the final impossibly high note, he threw his flute into the air. The spotlight left him and followed the flute arcing up toward the ceiling. When it reached its apex the last note stopped and the spotlight went out, plunging the hall back into darkness.

The stage exploded.

Three columns of flame shot straight up from the front of the stage and Brass Rat was there.

The electric guitar raged and drums pounded and the band kicked into one of their newer songs, "Pay the Piper" with its opening line: "So you say you wanna dance all night . . ."

5 · Ratter

Callie stood absolutely still watching the band, almost as if under an enchantment. Gringras' good looks—the high cheekbones, the thin nose, the brilliant green of his eyes— were mesmerizing. How could she have thought he was older than her father? He was simply beautiful, and he moved beautifully, too, like some great jungle cat, all oiled motion, flowing.

The drummer, Johnny Alabas, had some of that same beauty, but slightly tarnished. Everything about him was too sharp, too long, too white, as if he were a funhouse mirror reflection of the piper.

Bass player Tommy Nickels was small, compact, and dark. But it was the guitarist, Scott Morrison, who held Callie in thrall, with his long blonde hair tied back in a braid, his wide Viking face set with faded blue eyes. If Gringras was a cat, Scott was a horse. A stallion. Big and powerful and gorgeous. He was wearing black leather trousers with rats painted around the bottom of the legs, their tails twining up like strange vines. And a black tee with Celtic knotwork printed on front and back.

As she watched him, Callie felt something like an ache under her breastbone. She'd never felt like that before. *Is it love,* she wondered? Then shook her head. Her parents would never allow it.

"Aren't they brill!" Nick cried, meaning *brilliant,* the latest word in elementary school. It meant "great," "super," "the best." He tugged at Callie's sleeve.

She looked down at him and suddenly thought, *I'm standing with my little brother at a rock concert!* Her face flooded with embarrassed heat. Moving away quickly, she said, "Get lost, Peabrain. My friends are watching."

Then turning, she saw Alison and Josee and waved at them as the band segued into the next song, "Nobody Here But . . ."

Josee came over breathlessly, twining a black curl around one finger. Alison was right behind. "Whadda you think?" she began. "That Peter, that Gringras, the piper, he's . . . he's . . ."

Callie had never heard Josee stutter before. Usually she had a word or three for everything. But now she sounded dazed, almost as if she'd been hit over the head.

"Brill!" Callie said, before she remembered that was an elementary school word, and the heat flooded back into her face. "I mean, they're awesome."

"And your parents actually let you . . ." Alison began, reaching out to finger Callie's press pass.

Josee found her tongue again. "Yeah—your parents got the key and unlocked the door to your cage, let you loose.

Fly little bird, fly, Callifrage. Great going! But wasn't that the pea-brained little brother, Mr. Tittletattle Tagalong?"

About to answer back, Callie suddenly heard the music again, and found she couldn't keep still any longer. She started to dance circles around Alison and Josee, as if binding them to her. "Tell you *all*. Later," she said. Then off she went, skipping and hopping around the hall, her friends tagging after her, all three of them singing along with the music.

When the band broke into "Ratter, ratter, mad as a hatter . . ." they started to do the Ratter, a dance they'd learned from MTV. But it had been covered by the Blank Joves, and Callie was surprised to learn "Ratter" was a Brass Rat song. It hadn't been on any of the CDs her parents owned.

Scott led it off with a long descending riff on his guitar.

"SCOTT!" a number of the girls screamed out, and Callie whispered his name. As she did so, she felt a delicious shiver travel down her spine. *So this,* she thought, *is a major crush.* She'd never had one before. Then she surrendered to the feeling, throwing herself into the dance.

The dance went like this: One person was the Ratter and went sniffing around the other kids—the Rats—who danced hands down, then hands up, as if trying to get away.

> *"Hands down, or I'll swallow you whole,*
> *Hands up, do as you're told. . . ."*

When the band hit the line, "Give me money or I'll take your soul," the Ratter had to chose one of the dancers. Then the two proceeded to spin about together till the Ratter went down on to the floor. The Rat became the Ratter and it began all over again. If two Ratters met on the dance floor, though, they had to go Nose-to-Tail four times around, then spin off after other Rats.

Callie called out, "I'm Ratter!" the moment the guitar was over, which left Alison and Josee to join other Rats nearby.

AFTER RATTER, CALLIE AND ALISON and Josee just shuffled and shagged and jived through the next eight songs. They sweated up a storm but refused to stop, not even to get a drink of water.

Once Callie caught her dad's eye, and he winked at her. Another time she saw Nick who—with a bunch of his wee-nie friends—was dancing, too. If you could call what they did dancing. *Throwing themselves about was more like it,* Callie thought.

Then she saw her mother, right out there on the floor, where anyone could see her, doing a strange combination of bootie dancing and the Ratter, which was *so* embarrassing, Callie felt sick. She looked at the floor and thrust her hands down angrily, hoping that the floor could, as the lyrics said, swallow her whole.

Suddenly Gringras announced to the mike, "We're taking a short break. Don't go anywhere, you rats!" and the hall broke into a waterfall of applause.

Callie checked out her mother. She was nowhere in sight. Callie's knotted stomach seemed to ease.

"Want a soda, Callie?" Josee asked, her black curls now sorry-looking tangles. "They're selling all kinds of stuff out front, bottles, cans, plastic and paper cups. Drill them, fill them up."

"Merch, too," Alison added. She had two bright red spots on her cheeks, as if a child had colored them in with Magic Marker. "Tee shirts and headbands and hats and CDs and . . ." It was a long speech for her.

"Do they have hats?" Josee interrupted. "With little yellow rats on top? I saw one on someone. I'm dying to get one. And Peter's autograph. From his perfect fingers, down the pen, to me . . . to me . . . just for me." She started sputtering again.

Callie waved her press pass at them. "I'm going backstage for an interview. Hard work—but clearly somebody's got to do it."

"An interview?" Alison asked, voice squeaking, as if she'd never heard of Callie's plan. "With the *band*?"

Callie shook her head. "No, with the janitor." She made a face at them. "Of course with the band."

"And your parents are letting you all alone with those older men?" Josee said, her voice hovering between envy and astonishment. "What were they thinking, Califunny?"

"That I'm working?" Callie said. "Not shirking." She grinned, not needing to tell Josee how she managed it. *Let them think it was hard to do.*

"Can we come, too?" Josee asked. "Quiet as mice, not rats, and we'll be your backup, or your front down, whichever you want. Carry your pencils and pencil box, ma'am." Her fingers crawled all over her hair as she spoke.

Alison just looked eager.

"Press pass only covers one," Callie told them. "If you'd been in journalism class maybe you could have gotten one, too." Though she knew she was the only Hamp kid who'd wangled the assignment. "Get me a soda, will you?" She fished in her jeans pocket for a dollar. She wanted them to go before they found out she had to take Nick into the interview as the price of coming to the concert. The soda was a distraction, to get them out of the way while she rounded him up. "And don't worry about that interview. I'll give you the whole scoop later."

Alison looked beaten, her already thin lips thinning down into a line like the dash at the end of one of Emily Dickinson's poems. But Josee threatened another flood of words.

"Friends, my friend, don't . . ."

Holding out her little fingers, Callie interrupted saying, "Friends do pinkie promises."

First Alison, then Josee gripped her pinkies with theirs. "Pinkie promise," they both said, and Josee added, "You'd better, or the gods of journalism will dump their ink all over you, Callie, and it'll make your pumpkin head look like mine, jet-black and oily!"

Callie didn't answer, but spun away from them to find her parents and reclaim her notebook. And, she thought grimly, her pea-brained brother.

6 · Talk Is Cheap

And now, *the piper thought,* the part of this gig I've been dreading the most.

"Gringras!" Tommy shouted to him, already offstage and halfway down the hall. "Time to talk to the kids." He sounded thrilled by the prospect.

Gringras sighed, a deep theatrical affair. "If we must."

"We must if we want to get paid," said Alabas as he ignored the short set of stairs and leaped to the ground. "And we do need to get paid."

Gringras nodded. Talking to the children was better than the alternative. But he wasn't looking forward to it.

"Come," Alabas said, his voice softening. "We'll talk to them and get paid. Then we'll not have to see them again."

He almost sounds like the old Alabas there, *Gringras thought.* Like my friend.

Scott was the last down, his broad face lightly coated with sweat.

"What's up?" he asked, before answering himself. "Oh yeah, the school newspapers."

Gringras motioned the entire band down the hall toward the room where the interview would take place. He said nothing more. He was thinking of all of the children he'd had to talk to over the years. And those he'd had to "see again." Forever. Like the two princes.

"Thou art here to kill us, I wot," the older one had said matter-of-factly.

He'd looked so brave and fragile, standing guard over his younger brother, Gringras hadn't had the heart to tell him he was wrong.

7 · Interview

"Why are you guys called Brass Rat?" Nick blurted out when they'd gotten backstage and through a pus-colored door to the so-called "green room," though it was really painted black. They were there by the simple magic of waving the press pass.

Callie was horrified at Nick's outburst. She'd been trying to remain properly cool, as if she hung out in band rooms every day. The other school reporters from other high schools all laughed and nudged one another. And one guy, dressed in an actual jacket and tie, whispered, "Babysitter!" to the girl next to him.

Gringras ignored Mr. Tie and spoke directly to Nick in a kind of slow drawl. "Well, actually, there's an interesting and exciting story behind that." He didn't exactly lean forward from his position on the couch, but he seemed to slouch ever-so-slightly less. *Even up close, he didn't look old,* Callie thought. Unlike her father, who had lines around his eyes whenever he smiled, Gringras had a face that seemed smooth and flawless. And bored.

Maybe he's told this story too many times. Callie suddenly wondered whether this was how her article could start. *Maybe he's been around so long, nothing surprises him.* She liked that. It was what her journalism teacher called "a hook." She stood very still and listened carefully.

"It was years ago in an antique shop in Edinburgh," Gringras said.

"Edinburgh, Scotland?" Nick asked. "We studied that."

Callie rolled her eyes. *She* was the one supposed to do the interview. But how could she shut Nick up, short of putting a hand over his mouth?

Gringras smiled slowly and dropped into a Scottish brogue. "Aye, bonny Scotland." As quickly he dropped out, winking at Nick. "A shop near the North Sea. I saw, tucked way back on a high shelf, in the far back room of the shop, a rat as big as a small dog."

"A real rat?" Nick asked, leaning toward Gringras, leaning—Callie thought—into the story.

"No," Gringras replied, smiling at him, "it was made entirely of brass."

Callie suddenly realized that Gringras's actual accent was strange. It could have been from Eastern Europe; it could have been from England. If pressed, she would just have to call it: *foreign.*

"Well, I loved that brass rat at first sight. But what use could any sane man have for a big brass rat?" Gringras smiled again but—Callie thought—like a snake, without showing his teeth.

He leaned back against the sofa cushion. "I thought to myself, Gringras, you are not a rich man. But maybe, just maybe—since the silly-looking thing is tucked way back, on a high shelf, in the very back of the shop—then maybe I can make a bargain."

The school reporters all seemed mesmerized by the story, except for Callie who, pen poised over her notepad, waited for something real to write down. *Get on with it,* she begged him mentally. After all, her parents might want to see her notes. And right now there was nothing to show them.

"The shop owner and I haggled for hours," Gringras continued. "He claimed I was trying to beggar him and I screamed about shoddy workmanship. When he said I would starve his children if I forced him to go lower, I claimed I would not be able to afford a wife if I paid his asking price."

Wife? Callie thought. *I haven't read anywhere about a wife.* Now it was getting interesting. She jotted down *wife* with a question mark after it.

As if reading her thoughts, Gringras shook his head. "Always the price came down, down, down. When it was finally somewhere reasonable, well, I pulled out my wallet and bought myself one large brass rat."

The kids in the room breathed a long sigh, except for Callie.

I don't get it. The hand holding her notebook dropped to her side, but not so the other reporters. They were all madly scribbling on their pads. Mr. Tie had filled an entire page.

"I walked out of that store whistling and holding my new brass rat, buffing it with my coat sleeve," Gringras said, his voice getting lower as he spoke. Not lower, as if whispering, but lower in actual notes. He leaned forward again, too. "But fairly soon I noticed something strange. There seemed to be a large rat following me. And it was *not* made of brass. One very large, lean, and hungry-looking rat stalking me in broad daylight."

Callie drew in a ragged breath this time. She couldn't help herself.

"Well, this was strange," Gringras continued, "but it did not worry me overmuch. One rat is just not that frightening. But soon I saw another rat. And then another. And then . . . well, you see it coming."

The reporters all nodded, though only Callie really understood what Gringras was doing.

"Soon thousands upon thousands of rats were chasing me through the streets of Edinburgh! I ran and ran with a million rats behind me. And then I understood! They were after my rat. My big, beautiful brass rat. Now, I loved that brass rat! But I loved myself more. So I ran as fast as I could down to the Firth of Forth, which runs into the North Sea. And when I got there I threw that brass rat as far as I could." His arm made a huge arc as if he were throwing the rat at that very moment. In fact, he'd thrown an empty can that hit its intended target—the wastebasket—with a loud clang.

They all jumped at the sound.

Gringras continued the story as if the clanging can had been but a bit of punctuation. "The rats swarmed past me, paying me no mind. They charged into the river and climbed over each other in their frenzy to get to the brass rat. It was madness. They went to their deaths, drowned, every last mother's son of them." He paused and leaned slowly forward to grab another soda off the low table. Lifting it to his lips, he took a long drink.

Callie looked around the strangely silent room. The kids seemed stunned by the story—*the shaggy rat story,* she mentally dubbed it. However, she was more interested in how the band members were reacting and glanced at them each in turn out of the corner of her eye.

Scott sat restringing one of his guitars, yet was still listening intently. As Callie watched, his hands twitched and the end of a string punctured his index finger. A drop of blood sprang up from the wound. Scott ignored it and kept looking at Gringras.

Oh, Scott . . . she thought suddenly, the now-familiar ache in her stomach returning.

Tommy Nickels never glanced up from his science-fiction novel.

But Alabas sat stock-still, staring daggers at Gringras.

Gringras leaned back into the couch once more and spoke again. "When the carnage was over, I went back to the store where I had purchased the rat. I told my horrific story to the owner and he explained to me that no refunds would be given. 'No, no, you've got me all wrong,' I told him. 'All I want to know is . . .'" he paused for effect and winked at Nick, "'how much for that brass drummer there!'" He pointed at Alabas.

Nick erupted into laughter, which Gringras joined. Scott put down his guitar and took a long nervous pull from his drink. Alabas growled—actually growled—then stomped out of the room. Tommy Nickels still hadn't moved.

The school reporters seemed a bit startled that the story was just a joke. They stretched uneasily, then shot a series of questions at Gringras which he handled easily. Clearly he'd heard all the questions before.

At last he turned, grinned, and winked at Callie.

"Now, do you have any questions for me, young lady?"

Only then did he realize she was the only girl there.

"Um . . ." she said. It was not a good beginning.

"Did you ever get enough money for your wife?" Nick asked suddenly.

Callie flushed. Not because it was a stupid question. In fact it was on her own mental list. But to ask it so baldly. And in that way. And the implication that—since Nick was her little brother—she wanted to know the answer *especially* was too much.

"Nicky," she said, her voice low, "shut up or go away. Or both."

Gringras looked at her a moment, and it was as if only the two of them existed in all the world. His voice was soft, musical, low. "Be careful what you wish, my lady, for it might come true. And then you will have many years to rue it." He sighed, an uncharacteristic sound. "As I know all too well." Then he turned to the others. "Interview over. Time for the second half. Hope you like the show."

Before they knew what had happened, they were all back in the hall and the band was playing "Green in the Haven," a fast and furious reel.

What was that about? Callie asked herself. *Be careful what you wish and all that? Any fool knows wishes don't come true.* If they did, she'd have parents who were less strict, a name like Elizabeth, her brother Mars at a school closer to home, and a boyfriend who looked a lot like Scott. *A lot!*

But the music had some kind of power that overtook her. Dancing to it, Callie let the music wash over her until it had stopped her thinking altogether.

> *"Green in the haven,*
> *Green in the bower,*
> *Green in the wide wold world all over."*

8 · Exile

Gringras hunched over his flute, improvising madly. Brass Rat was well into its ten-minute final encore, "Exile," and the chord changes were coming fast and furious. Still, Gringras let his mind wander as his fingers danced across his instrument. The band was in disarray. He could feel the tension between the members like a physical weight on the music.

He knew why. The approaching teind had him uneasy. And when he was uneasy, he made the others downright uncomfortable.

Turning, he glanced at Alabas, who stared down at his own feet, grimly striking his drums.

He's still angry, *thought Gringras.* All these years and I can still prick his pride with an old joke or an off word.

He signaled the others and spun in place, coming to rest with his flute in his left hand pointing at Scott, who took over the solo.

Scott was another problem altogether. Judging by his reaction to the Brass Rat story, he was beginning to suspect something. It was getting time to tell him everything or cut him loose.

And if he is cut loose, *Gringras thought,* he can't be left to walk around. Not in the condition he would be in then.

He sighed. Threes, *he thought,* trouble comes in threes. If Alabas' pride is one, and Scott's suspicions makes two, then what is the third? The third is always the killer.

Scott had begun an intricate run of triplets that signaled the end of his solo. Gringras raced over to the opposite side of the stage and Tommy Nickels shotgunned him with the bass and grinned.

No problem there, *thought Gringras, returning the grin with as much warmth as he could muster. He couldn't remember the last time Tommy had spoken more than a single sentence, let alone voiced an opinion or caused a problem. He had only two loves—music and sci-fi. The rockets and ray-guns kind.* I can always count on little Tommy.

The pyrotechnics flared again and more explosions rocked the hall. The audience screamed with delight and Gringras sprinted to center stage in time to sing a reprise of the chorus.

"Time and place mean nothing if you can't call them home."

The crowd sang with him, holding their hands up pinkie and forefinger extended. To them it meant "Go for it! Great! Brill!" To him, it was his father's sign. The way he had held his hand up when he'd sent Gringras out into the world.

Gringras smiled his mocking snake smile at them all, thinking: This gig will easily cover the remainder of the teind, and Alabas will soon recover from whatever slight to his pride I have delivered. He always does.

"Born of man and woman, you do not walk alone."

And Scott . . . he will either accept things as they truly are or he will be dealt with in turn.

"Me, I stalk the darkness, each solitary mile."

Nothing to worry about then, *he thought. But he wasn't convincing himself. There was something different this time. Something even he, with his farsight, was not seeing.*

"Apart but not far distant—Exile!"

9 · More Curses

Callie was so caught up in the music, she forgot that "Exile" was the final piece Brass Rat played in each concert. Or so the Internet reviews had said. So when the last note died away and the lights went down, then came up again on an empty stage, she felt empty, too.

That was when she remembered that Peter Gringras had never answered the one question her readers would really want to know. Well, her *girl* readers, anyway. *What about this wife? What's this about a payment?* She bit her lip. Was that one question or two?

Shrugging, she spun around, looking for her parents in the crowd. She finally spotted them leaning against the far wall, looking spent. Nick stood in front of them, waving his hands at her frantically, like a sailor on a sinking ship waving flags.

Callie walked quickly to them, ignored Nick, and said, "I have one more question I have to ask the band."

"We need to go," her dad said. "Your mom's pooped."

Her mother interrupted. "Your dad's the one who's done. Not as young as we once were."

Running his right hand through his hair, her dad leaned forward and said, "What more do you need to ask them? You were in there for at least half an hour."

"A half is not a whole," Callie said, immediately regretting her snarky tone. So she added, "This is for *school*, Dad."

"Make it quick then," her dad said.

"We'll meet you outside," her mom added.

Nick's eyes brightened. "Can I come?"

"Not this time."

"Mommmmmmy . . ." he began, but Callie was gone.

Pushing past a long line of people waiting for a chance at the unisex bathroom, Callie found her way back to the band room. She waved her press pass, and was about to go inside when she realized the door was ajar. She could hear angry voices coming from within.

One belonged to Gringras. "What is this? What does this mean—a freebie?" He spoke like a snake, low, hissing.

"Look," came the rough growling answer, "I already told your manager that . . ."

"I *am* the manager," Gringras said. There was real menace in his voice.

"I thought the manager's name was Lola Kudnohofski," the man complained.

"I use that name when dealing with creeps like you, Garner," Gringras said. "It saves face all around."

"What's this about saving face?" the man demanded.

Gringras was silent.

Callie thought a minute about barging in, decided against it, but that didn't stop her from listening at the door. *A reporter,* she told herself, *has a duty to her readers.* Besides, her parents would ask what was said. . . .

"Look, here's the letter, and the contract—which you signed—and it clearly says this is a concert to raise money for the homeless," the growly man added.

"And just as clearly I—or rather Lola—told you that we would come but would expect to be paid our normal rate. Not a percentage of the gate, not an advance on future earnings, but our normal rate. In cash. Now."

Callie heard a chair being shoved back. Someone was standing up. If anyone left the room now, the door would hit her in the ear. That would be tough to explain! But if she left, she'd never know—and could never report—how this whole thing ended. She pressed herself back against the wall. Now if the door opened, she would be behind it and invisible to anyone exiting.

"Pay us the money, the gold and silver we worked for," Gringras continued. "We need it tonight. Not tomorrow. Tomorrow will be too late."

Callie heard something else in Gringras's voice. It sounded like a wild pleading and a threat, both at the same time.

"*All* the funds go to the homeless. That's the way it is." The man spoke as if he made the rules. "*All* funds."

Then Gringras said something really odd. "I *am* the homeless. More so than you can ever know." He threw the door open, completely shutting Callie from view, and stomped off, his boots making a resounding noise.

The door shut again, partway, and Callie took a deep

breath, ready now to declare herself. But Alabas' voice from the band room stopped her. He was saying something that made no sense, his voice rising louder and louder until he was thundering:

"May ye gae thru mirk and mire,
Fill your breeks with muck of byre.
Wade through blude, and walk the gyre,
And ne'er come hame till I desire."

What he was saying sounded English or Scottish or both. Like Callie's Scottish gran when she really got going. A few of the words were even ones Gran used. *Breeks,* meaning "pants" or "breeches." *Blude,* meaning "blood." The whole thing, though, was both like a song and like a curse and like nothing Callie had ever heard before. She shivered and the hair on the back of her neck stood up.

"Look, Mr. Garner," this time it was Scott speaking, "Alabas is just riled. Don't pay any attention to him."

But Alabas kept going, and Callie got that shivery feeling all over again.

"Walk abroad until ye tire,
Head and hair and heart afire,
Round aboot the dread dear's spire,
And ne'er come hame till I desire."

"Crazy musicians," Garner growled, and then he, too, stomped off, throwing the door open, which once again blocked Callie.

"Now look what you've done," Scott said, clearly speaking to Alabas.

"What *I've* done?" Alabas laughed, but there was no humor in it. "You still do not understand, Scott. Twenty-one years with us, and you do not understand."

Actually it was Callie who didn't understand. *Twenty-one years Scott had been with the band?*

She tried to remember her research. If he'd been with the band for twenty-one years, he'd been there from the beginning, though not—she recalled—Tommy. Suddenly something that should have puzzled her before leaped out at her. Scott was maybe twenty, though he looked Callie's age. Or a year or two older. Yet if he'd joined the band twenty-one years ago. She thought about this. He'd have had to have been fifteen at least then. Maybe sixteen. Plus twenty-one. She did the math. Gulped, Did it again. That *couldn't* be right.

"Tomorrow is All Hallows' Eve and he needs that money to make up the teind."

"Yeah, I know, I know." Scott sounded almost bored. "Every seven years and he has to send money—*our* money—back home. Or else. Though no one ever says what the or-else is. And he makes it up to us after, so who cares."

"I care," Alabas retorted. "You do *not* understand."

"Try me. My God, Alabas, after all this time, at least *try* me."

There was a deep intake of breath, then Alabas said, "He must send silver or gold or souls Under the Hill. Human souls. To pay off a blood guilt, a teind. And if he does not, he will grow old as any who walks upon the earth instead of living long Under the Hill. He will grow old and then die himself. Do you believe Gringras would let such a thing happen?"

"Hey—we all die. In time."

Alabas laughed. It was not an easy laugh and there was no humor in it.

At that Scott was silent. A deep, long silence.

Callie had no way of knowing if he was silent because he knew that what Alabas was saying was crazy, or if he was just about to laugh at the joke, or . . . Because nothing Alabas had just said made any sense.

Callie turned over the words in her mind: Silver. Gold. Human souls. Blood guilt.

What is Alabas talking about?

And where is Under the Hill?

Then all of a sudden it made a kind of bizarre sense, ugly and scary. Like a horror movie the moment after you get the plot.

Only, Callie told herself, *this is real life in Northampton, Massachusetts, not some mad Hollywood concoction. Not one of Granny Kirkpatrick's fairy tales which used to scare me out of sleeping. Not watching some dumb TV show while Mars made spooky commentaries.*

Yet somehow Callie believed Alabas. Believed what he was saying. Believed him down in the urpy part of her stomach. And afraid she was going to be sick, she slipped away and ran out the nearest door marked EXIT.

SHE FOUND HERSELF IN A small, dark alley behind the theater. An over-full Dumpster seemed to be vomiting up beer cans and Coke bottles and paper trash. The place smelled strange, old, damp, unhealthy.

Hearing the sound of a flute, she looked up.

Gringras was sitting on the fire escape above her, his legs dangling down. He was playing a sort of doleful version of "Ratter." Down below him some movement drew her eye.

Three brown rats were standing on their hind legs and dancing in a circle, paw-to-paw-to-paw, chittering.

Callie gasped, and turned to go back inside the theater, but the door had shut silently behind her and there was no handle on the outside.

Gringras must have heard her gasp, for he took the flute from his lips and started to laugh, a hollow sound not unlike Alabas' laugh, and it sent a cold chill down her spine.

The rats dropped paws, went down on all fours, and scattered, their little claws making a *scritching* sound as they fled.

For a long moment Callie couldn't move. It was as if she had lead weights on her arms and legs. As if she were encased in a cement body suit. And then, suddenly, she was released and she ran straight past the fire escape and Gringras' awful laughter, into a side street that led around to the front of the theater.

There she saw her parents.

"Mom!" she cried. "Dad!"

They gathered her up in comforting arms. "Got the rest of the story?" they asked in one voice, as they often did.

She didn't even have the strength to nod.

10 · Souls

The rats scattered, the girl gone, Gringras' laughter died in his throat. He put his flute to his lips and blew one high, petulant note.

But for men like Garner . . . *he began but let the thought die unfinished. Time to get to work. For a tithe of this scope, there were preparations to be made. And only a night and a day to make ready.*

Gringras sighed and got to his feet. He gazed down the alley where the girl had disappeared. No need to chase her, *he thought,* she will be gathered up with the rest of the children soon enough.

"Silver, gold, or souls," his father, the king, had cursed him so many years ago. And all to be earned by the sweat of his brow—a cruel joke that. His father had never considered whether that was going to be enough for him to earn the exorbitant cost of the teind every seven years in the human world. Gringras stuck out his lower lip, turning his handsome face into a mask. He knew he had a small talent for music. And he was

clever. He still had some of the powers of an exiled prince of Faerie. But those hadn't been enough. Not even at the beginning. By the end of the first six years of exile, he had found himself broke.

For the first time.

And not the last.

He remembered that awful year, A.D. 1212 by mortal count. He had been living in Germany with Alabas, for Alabas had refused to let him go into the human world alone.

"I am yours, my prince," Alabas had said, kneeling and taking the blood oath to bind them, and doing so in front of the king.

Gringras remembered laughing. He had been so confident then. "Then you will sweat along with me, my best of friends?"

Alabas had smiled.

Predictably, the king had been furious, but the oath was already sworn. And the curse. He could undo neither. That was the trouble with oaths and curses. Each had to run its course.

Gringras and Alabas went into exile, though nobody really wished it, and all of Faerie mourned.

However, the "sweat of his brow" had barely been enough to earn them food and lodgings. When that first seventh year was fast approaching, they were making music and a meager living in Germany. Looking into their pockets, they realized with horror that they had not enough silver. Not enough gold. It was time then to look into the third option.

Souls.

The souls had to be alive, not dead, of course. Dead they went elsewhere, where even Gringras could not follow. No, the souls they collected had to be alive and kept happy all the way down the long, twisting trail, across the river of blood, and into Faerie where they would live forever, dancing attendance on the king.

That first attempt was a huge failure. It seemed that adults were resistant to the lure of faerie music . . . and they were generally armed as well. The men Gringras and Alabas tried to enchant for the long walk into Faerie had turned on them with knives and pitchforks, cudgels and stakes. Despite the popular belief of the day, cold iron didn't kill his kind, but it certainly left Alabas half-dead, and Gringras incapacitated for some time.

And time was another thing they had very little of.

Gringras knew that if he missed the teind—so his father's curse went—he would never be allowed back into Faerie and would eventually die the true death in the human world. As would Alabas, his sworn blood brother.

"We must leave Germany and try France," Gringras had told Alabas, thinking: The French are great music lovers. We will find the souls we need there. *They stumbled away from the field where the Germans had left them to die.*

Gringras remembered walking the road, Alabas at his side, the two of them hungry and thirsty—and quarreling. Under the Hill they had never quarreled. But on the roads of earth, Alabas had learned regret early—and spite.

Near Marseilles, they met towheaded Nicolas of Germany and pockmarked Stephen of France, two boys with a grand plan. They were leading a ragtag band of children to the Holy Land.

"The Children's Crusade," Stephen called it, his voice high as a girl's for it had not broken yet.

"These will do," Alabas had said under his breath.

"Not children," Gringras answered him plaintively, though he knew they were his only hope. "Not children." Regret first. Spite came after.

With the help of Gringras' pipe and Alabas' hand drum—and not a few spells spoken in the guise of Christian prayers—the small band of children grew to thousands. And if some number of the children disappeared with Gringras and Alabas before ever reaching Jerusalem, well, they were probably better off then those who took Hugh the Iron's offer of transportation.

Hugh sold those poor, deluded children into slavery.

Death in life.

Whereas the children Under the Hill were still alive centuries later.

Life in death.

11 · Homework

Callie barely slept that night, but in her dreams she danced Ratter up one alley and down the next followed by a group of kids dressed in leather and calling themselves Brown Norways.

Getting up early, she determined to go right to school. There was a lot of research that still needed doing before she could get her story down. Since her parents had child protection wards on their computer, that ruled out a lot of the really helpful sites. Rock and roll was not for babies!

She was still going to write that article for the school paper, all right. But not the one everyone was expecting. Not a puff piece about the great band, or whether Gringras had a wife or not.

This one was going to be about rats—the real biting kind.

It was going to be about mirk, mire, gyres, and blood guilt.

It was going to be about Under the Hill, wherever that was.

And the teind, whatever that was.

It was going to rock her school and, possibly, win her an award. And all this was good—if only she could forget the rats.

Callie raced downstairs and was just gulping down a glass of milk and snarfing down a Pop-Tart when Nick came into the kitchen.

"That was brill, last night, didn't you think so, Cal?" His eyes were wide open, though the left still had a bit of sleep sand there and he rubbed at it with his fist.

"It was . . . *something* all right," she mumbled, grabbing up her backpack and heading for the door. Shouting over her shoulder, she said, "Let Mom know I've gone to school already. That should surprise her."

Nick stood in the doorway in his Batman jammies, waving. He seemed small, vulnerable, unprotected from the wind. Callie looked at him with affection. She always liked him a lot better when she got away from his side. For a moment she wondered if Mars had felt the same about her.

School was strangely silent because only a few homeroom teachers and the janitor—a surly man named Jamsie—were there so early. Callie smiled. Who would have believed it? Without the buzz, the bells, the yells, the clanging of locker doors, school was actually a place where a person could think.

Heading toward the journalism room, she thought about where she would start working on her article. The word *teind* was unfamiliar to her. Perhaps that was what she needed to know first.

But how to spell it?

Signing in on the computer's dictionary, she brought up

tined and *tinned.* She tried *tiend,* but there was nothing between Tien Shan—which was a mountain range in Central Asia—and tiepin.

Biting her lip, she went on to Google.

Even Google was puzzled.

Finally she stood up and walked over to the bookshelf where the dictionaries stood stiffly like unhappy siblings in a row on the top.

The American dictionaries said nothing helpful, but when she took out the *Oxford English Dictionary*—what her journalism teacher liked to call "the last port in a storm"—she found by accident that the word was spelled *teind.*

"That just plain looks wrong!" she said aloud, mouthing *I before e except after c. . . .*

It seemed that *teind* meant a "tithe," which was something they did in Callie's church, so at least she knew the meaning without having to look that up as well. In church *to tithe* meant "to give a part of one's income, a kind of tax, for good causes." She remembered how Alabas had said something about paying a blood guilt. So maybe they were talking about some kind of payment that involved guilt. Blood guilt. That seemed to fit. She still didn't like the way the word looked, though: *e before i.* Shrugging, she closed the dictionary and turned back to the computer.

"What looks wrong?" It was Josee, hand twisting her hair, a black curl around a finger looking like a dark ring. "And why are *you* here so early? Nobody in their right mind gets here this early, middle of the night, before dawn's early light."

"You're here and I bet you're in your right mind," Callie

retorted. "As for me, I'm left-brained and writing that article about the concert."

"Mom had to go to work early and dropped me." Josee's mother was a nurse. "Last time she had an early shift, I slept through the alarm. She said it wasn't going to happen again. Therefore, I am zonked, out of it, in the *zzzz* place, without a top floor. Like I said, nobody in their right mind . . ." She slung her backpack on top of Callie's. "So what looks wrong?"

"This word." Callie typed it onto the computer.

"I before e except after c," Josee recited. "An eternal truth, according to V. Louise." Their English teacher.

"I know, I know. But that's how it's spelled."

"What's it mean when it's home on its own? Give me something, Callifunny."

Callie made a face. "A tithe, a payment of some sort."

"A payment? For what?" Josee leaned over, her nose almost touching the monitor. She was tremendously nearsighted and hated to wear her glasses. Her mother had vetoed lenses till she was sixteen. And pierced ears. Both of which Josee felt were tremendously unfair.

"For blood guilt, is what I heard."

Josee laughed. "And what's *that* mean, Calli-bean?"

"What's *what* mean?" It was Alison. She was usually the first of them at school, catching up on homework she forgot to do the night before, so neither of them were surprised to see her.

"Blood guilt," said Josee just as Callie said, "Teind."

"Oh, I know that one!" Alison said.

"Which one?" they asked together.

"*Teind.* It's in a song Daddy sings." Her father was a folksinger, only modestly successful, or so Callie's parents said, meaning he was known best in Western Massachusetts and played at bars and clubs around the area. Alison quoted him all the time. "A real dote-head instead of a daughter," is what Josee called her, out of Alison's hearing. But then Alison didn't have a mother, so Callie always cut her a lot of slack.

"What song?

"It's called 'Tam Lin.' " Alison began to sing in a quavery voice:

"All pleasant is the fairy land
For those that in it dwell,
But at the end of seven years
They pay a teind to hell;
And I'm so fair and full of flesh,
I'm feared twill be mysel'."

Callie's heart seemed to stutter. *Seven years!* That was exactly what Scott had said. *This thing is sounding more and more like one of Granny's stories, with magic and elves and . . .*

"But what about blood guilt?" Josee was asking. "Sounds extremely yucky, not to mention unsanitary, unappetizing, unappealing, and certainly unsafe."

"Dunno anything about that," Alison said. "What do you think?"

"I'd feel guilty about spilling blood, I guess. Not to mention grossed out, finger-down-the-throat gagged, and totally incapacitated with the mewling poos!"

They kept nattering on, but Callie barely heard them.

Her mind was suddenly filled with questions: What had she stumbled into? Was it the Mafia? Or gang payments? Or a drug cartel? Or . . . Suddenly she remembered the rats dancing.

"Rats!" she said aloud.

Just then a bell rang.

School had started and her friends had been hardly any help at all.

CALLIE HAD TROUBLE CONCENTRATING IN algebra. The logarithms she'd understood only the week before now made no sense. In her Earth Science class, she kept confusing the Jurassic with the Mesozoic, much to her teacher's annoyance. And in her English class—usually her best subject—she was well behind the class reading of *A Day No Pigs Would Die*, which she thought was a stupid book anyway. When she said so aloud, V. Louise looked daggers at her and she could feel her grade sinking with each word.

In fact, the entire day, all she could think about was the band and the odd things Alabas had been saying to Scott. Visions of the dancing rats kept coming back to her. Each time she saw Alison and Josee, they asked her questions about the "blood guilt" which she couldn't answer.

"Maybe it's blood *gilt*," Josee said at lunch, "like gilding the lily, adding gold, painting by the numbers."

"That makes no sense at all," remarked Alison, which was the first sensible thing anyone had said about it all day.

Callie picked up her tray and walked away from the table,

pointedly ignoring them both. After all, *they* hadn't heard Alabas, hadn't seen the dancing rats.

Rats! She grew obsessed with them. By the last period, the three rats in the alley had grown in her mind to several thousands, much as they had in Gringras' silly story. And Josee and Alison were no longer speaking to her.

Which, Callie told herself, *is just as well as they aren't saying anything of interest.*

Her last class was Spanish.

Señora Bastanada had asked something simple, but Callie's mind wandered back again to last night. She could almost hear the piping of Gringras' flute, could smell the dark, close, garbage-strewn alley, could feel the shiver of cold along her spine.

"Señorita McCallan," the teacher was saying, but Callie didn't hear her until the third time. *"¿Callie McCallan, dónde esta usted?"*

Callie looked up to see everyone staring at her, and said the first thing that came into her head. "Rats! Dirty rats!"

"En Español, por favor."

She thought a minute. *"¿Ratons con manos negres?"*

Everyone laughed. Even Señora Bastanada.

The bell saved her from a detention, and she hurried back to the journalism room, determined to write the story—rats and all.

Suddenly she remembered an old poem about the Pied Piper of Hamelin which her mother used to recite: *"Rats! They fought the dogs and killed the cats, and bit the babies in the cradles, and ate the cheeses out of the vats. . . ."* Not a fairy tale after all.

"That's it!" she said aloud. Now she knew where the story would start. Not just with the band, but with the rats.

Lots of rats.

She signed in on the computer, put her name at the top, and began.

Calcephony McCallan
HAMELIN COMES AGAIN
Last night, the Pied Piper came to the Valley. His name is Peter Gringras. But who will pay the piper this time?

It may seem strange, impossible even, but what if Peter Gringras, that rock-and-roll legend, is really the Pied Piper? Not of Northampton, but of Hamelin.

That's right, Hamelin. Remember the rats?

She printed out what she had, read it over, and sighed. "I've lost my stupid mind," she whispered, crumpling up the paper and two-pointing it into the waste basket. It gave her no pleasure. "How can I be so gullible?" she said knowing that the dictionary would say that *gullible* meant "easily fooled." It was one of Mars' favorite words.

Then she put her head in her hands. The memory of the three little brown rats made her sit up again. She turned back to the computer, got onto Google again, and this time looked up *Hamelin*. There was stuff about the legend and stuff about the real place. Those articles sent her to sites about the Children's Crusade, the little princes in the tower, about other kinds of missing children, faces on milk bottles, the Atlanta child murders, and lots about child abuse. None of it was pleasant reading. She was sorry she'd gotten involved.

Erasing the two paragraphs she'd already written, she started again.

Last night, a Pied Piper came to the Valley. His name is Peter Gringras. He and his band, Brass Rat, played their hearts out for over 5,000 appreciative fans.

Then rock legend Gringras found himself stiffed by the concert promoter after the gig. He was not paid what his contract called for. So will he, like the Pied Piper in the old story, take out his anger not on the rats but on the children of Northampton . . .

She couldn't figure out where to go from there. It certainly wasn't journalism, but a kind of bizarre fiction. No one would put it in the school paper this way. Nor did she think it belonged there. It made no sense, no proper sense. It was about mystery, magic, and leaps of faith. Journalism had to be about real things, about facts.

So, she printed out what she had, including all the bits of research she'd gleaned from the Google search, closed her eyes, and tried to think.

But all she could think was: *My parents are going to kill me if I write this and get a D for Dumb and Dumber.*

"I'll call Mars," she told herself. Even when her parents ignored her, or got on her case, Mars could be counted on. "He'll know what to do."

12 · Tricks or Treats

Callie was still sitting with her eyes closed when Jamsie the janitor came into the room. He wasn't very quiet about it, setting his mop pail down with a bang.

"Whatcha doin, Carrot Top?" he growled. His tone sounded threatening though the words were not.

Callie looked up and saw him scowling at her. His wild white hair seemed even less combed than usual. She'd never liked him, especially because he always called her Carrot Top.

"Thinking," she said.

"Well, do yer thinking some'ere else," he snarled. "I gotta clean up here. "'Sides, school isn't no place for thinking." He shook the mop at her.

Suddenly she realized that she and Jamsie were probably the only two people left in the school, and that he could easily murder her, cut her up, and hide the pieces in his broom closet with no one the wiser.

Right, she thought, *scare yourself silly over a bad-tempered janitor. Like this is* Friday the 13th *or some other dumb movie.*

Clearly, fiction was becoming her new way of thinking.

She grabbed up the beginning of her article and her book bag, then left the school almost at a run. She'd hate to have her parents tell the police, "We told her so." It didn't occur to her, until she was two blocks away and pedaling fast, what Jamsie had said.

"School isn't no place for thinking!" she repeated, and then began laughing so hard, she almost went right past her street.

"Calcephony McCallan, where *have* you been?" her mother began the moment Callie walked in. "I was about ready to call the police."

"Doing homework, Mom. At school."

"School is no place for homework . . ." her mother said.

Callie laughed. "The janitor just said something like that. He said school was no place for thinking. . . ."

"Don't get smart with me, young . . ." Her finger was pointing at Callie.

"But, Mom, I'm *agreeing* with you."

Her mother took a moment, then laughed with her. "You're right. Must be last night's excitement and lack of sleep. I was just worried you wouldn't get back in time."

"Back in time for dinner? Do I ever miss a meal?" Callie asked.

"Back in time for trick-or-treating."

Callie mentally thwacked her head with the palm of her hand. How could she have forgotten? She'd promised to take Nick out this year because Mom and Dad were going off to a Halloween party themselves. How surprised and happy she'd been when they proposed it. Finally they were letting her off the leash. Well, at least loosening the leash a little. After all, she and Nick would be out with all the other neighborhood kids.

Plunging her hand into her backpack, Callie pulled out the paper with the two paragraphs and waved it in front of her mother's eyes. "Two paragraphs! That's all I've got so far, Mom. And it's due tomorrow."

Her mother put her head to one side and gave Callie the you-should-have-known-better look. "Then you should have started earlier."

Callie was ready to cry. "It's the article about last night's concert, Mom. I couldn't have started it any earlier. That's why I stayed after school. I was trying my hardest to get it done because I'd promised Nicky I'd take him tonight. Only, you see, I can't. And I wanted to. . . . I *really* wanted to."

Her mother gave her a considering look. "Oh—that article. Well, you tried, Callie, and that's what's important."

Callie knuckled her eyes to get rid of the tears. She hated crying. It made her face splotchy. A redhead with splotches was the worst!

"So finish your paper, and I'll get the Piatts to take him. But no leaving the house." This time she put her finger up to emphasize what she was saying. It was like an exclamation point.

Suddenly grinning, Callie gave her mom a hug. "You're the greatest!"

"Well . . ."

"Oh—and I need to call Mars."

"Now?"

"I need his help on the paper."

Her mother looked at her with a strange expression on her face, part annoyance and part hurt. "Can't I help?"

"It's a . . . thing about magic and mystery, Mom."

"That's Mars all right." Shrugging, her mother went up the stairs. "Dinner in an hour. Right now I have to turn myself into a witch."

Callie resisted the obvious and went to the phone. Dialing the frat house, she told the boy who answered that she wanted to speak to Mars McCallan.

"So does everybody," he said. Then he shouted Mars' name loud enough to blast Callie's ears.

When Mars took the phone, Callie plunged in without any explanation. "It's bizarre and strange, and scary, too," she said.

"Whoa, little sister, make it fast. I have a Halloween party to run." Then he laughed. Mars always laughed, a waterfall of sound.

"There's this rock group—the Brass Rat. . . ."

"I know them. Rock and reel. 'Exile' is a real existential anthem."

"Define *existential*?" She hated not knowing what things meant.

"You'll need to take Philosophy 101 when you get to college." He laughed again. "The dictionary definition just won't do."

She sat on the bottom step of the stairs and wound the long phone cord around her hand. Her parents refused to get a cordless. They said it only encouraged people to lose the phone. "This is not a joke, Mars. I saw dancing rats, and they take souls, and . . ."

"Happy Halloween, Sis," he said. "Thanks for the trick. Though it makes no sense. I'll send you a treat later. Got a couple hundred people about to arrive in costume and me not even dressed yet. I'm going as Oberon. You know—the fairy king." And he hung up.

Callie stared at the phone for a long moment. The buzz it made was so much like a raspberry, she was surprised the phone didn't stick out a tongue at her.

How can Mars do that? she wondered. *How can he treat me that way?* He had always been her champion, her white knight. He was the one who put Band-Aids on her scrapes and kept the bullies away. And now his stupid party was more important than . . . than . . .

Than what? Her fictions? Callie shook her head, hung up the phone, and went up the stairs. Once in her room she entered the two paragraphs she'd written in school into her computer.

They didn't look any better.

Or any worse.

DINNER WAS A STRANGE AFFAIR. Her father was dressed like Harry Potter, with a wizard's pointy hat and a lightning bolt over his right eyebrow. But otherwise he was still in a business suit.

"Harry grown-up," he explained. "Though I'll also have a robe. And boots."

"And be stifling," Callie said.

"Just warm," he retorted.

Her mother as a witch was even weirder. She'd applied green makeup to her face and hands. Some of it had come off on the macaroni and cheese.

"Vegetable dye, I hope," Callie muttered, pushing some of the greener pieces to the side of her plate.

Nick was having trouble keeping his wizard sleeves out of his bowl. He was a smaller version of his father, but the sleeves seemed large enough for both of them. Callie left the table, found two rubber bands, and made him cuffs.

"Thanks, Cal," he said, looking up at her with adoration. *Probably,* she thought, with a twist of her mouth, *the same way I used to look up at Mars. Who dumped me to play the fairy king.*

"Sorry I can't do the big T&T with you, Bugbrain," she told him. "You sure look . . . magical."

He beamed.

"The Piatt kids will be by in fifteen minutes, Nick," the witch said. "We'll be gone, but Callie will be here when you get back."

"And not a minute past eight o'clock," said the big Harry Potter, adjusting his hat. "Then off to bed."

Nick nodded. "Can I have one piece of candy then?"

"Just one," the witch and the old Potter said together.

"Or you'll be flying higher than a witch without a broom!" added Mom, and punctuated it with a cackle.

"Remember that, Calcephony," her father intoned and waved his wand. "Eight o'clock is pumpkin time for this little wizard."

"Honestly," Callie said, as she excused herself from the table and headed upstairs, "this has to be the weirdest family in the entire world."

She was to remember that later. Much later. When she longed for their small strangeness in the midst of a much greater one.

13 · Casting

In a small wooded copse atop a large hill, Gringras had cleared an area to work. Lit candles stood at the five corners and a small brazier sputtered and sparked in the center.

As he skipped and danced, playing his flute, shadows from the flickering lights painted mad caricatures of him in the tree-tops. Woodland creatures—rabbits and squirrels and brown-eyed does—gathered around the clearing, their eyes glowing in the darkness.

Gringras reflected on how he had come to this predicament, this earthly place. How he, a minstrel prince of Faerie, could be reduced to a wandering busker, singing for his supper. How he, a magician of some skill, had ended up in this magic-less land, trying to cast any spell of note. How he, once a powerful prince, had become lower then the meanest bogie, who at least has the good taste to leave a changeling in place of the children it steals.

Gringras danced and played.

And remembered.

HE REMEMBERED THE WARM SPRING *day—like most of the days in Faerie—when he decided to kill his older brother.*

Gringras had two brothers: Tormalas was older, and Wynn was younger, putting Gringras in the middle. He had neither the power of the older brother nor the freedom of the younger. The middle billy goat gruff, *he thought. He followed humbly in their footsteps, a dutiful sibling, until he would finally fade into obscurity, munching on the good green grass on the other side of the bridge.*

Gringras had no wish to fade into obscurity.

But, in Faerie, stories have real power. It is, after all, the birth-place of faerie tales. He knew the form: Oldest sons stay home to inherit kingdoms from wise kings and go on to become wise kings themselves. Youngest sons have grand adventures where they out-wit dragons and demons and save princesses to marry so they, too, can eventually inherit kingdoms and become wise old kings.

Middle sons, *Gringas thought crankily,* middle sons chew grass.

He sat cross-legged on a small rise overlooking a field of pur-ple and red flowers, chewing on a wheat stalk like a human farm boy. Tiny feylings hovered above the colorful blossoms, their miniature wings buzzing furiously.

"What say you, Gringras?"

Gringras jumped. He had been so deep in thought he had not noticed Alabas coming up behind him. Gringras spit the wheat stalk out and stood up with what dignity he could muster.

"What say I?" Gringras replied, "I say we change our des-tiny." He spoke firmly and frowned when Alabas laughed.

"Big thoughts for such a warm, lazy day, my prince. I thought we were destined to eat lunch. I would not want to change that!"

Gringras' mood broke and he laughed, clapping his friend on the back.

"We will not change that part of it, Alabas. But let me tell you of my thoughts while we eat."

A short time later, their appetites sated, Gringras laid out his murderous plan.

"If we get caught," Alabas mused, "I cannot imagine the punishment we will receive."

"We will not *get caught, my friend. And besides," Gringras winked, "my brother will only be dead for a short time."*

"Just long enough?" asked Alabas.

"And no longer." Gringras was now as sunny as the day.

14 · Eight O'Clock Warning

Once the Piatt kids had come to pick up Nick—with many loud promises of getting him back by eight—the house quieted somewhat. Every once in a while, though, her mother's high, witchy cackle or her father's shout of "Where did I leave that wand?" broke through Callie's concentration.

Since her parents promised to leave a big tub of candy at the door with a sign saying **HERE'S THE TREAT!** Callie didn't have to go down to feed the princesses and wizards and elves who visited their front porch. The tub had been her mother's idea.

Sometimes, Callie thought, *parents can be cool.* Though when she thought about it some more, she realized it was less cool than meant to keep her from the door and possible danger.

Danger! she thought. Nothing dangerous or even anything slightly weird ever happened at her house; her parents wouldn't allow it. Except . . . She shuddered, then remembered that the dancing rats and Alabas' strange poem and the teind had all happened at the concert, not at her house. Shrugging, she sat down at her desk, content that she wouldn't be bothered by anything else. Then she put on her earphones and grooved to an Eric Clapton CD she'd taken from her father's collection.

She stared at the computer screen and the paragraphs she'd put there.

And stared.

And stared.

And stared some more.

Nothing came to her. Not an idea. Not another sentence. Not a noun or verb or dependent clause.

Not a *reason*.

Nothing.

Twice her hand strayed toward the phone, ready to call her older brother. Twice she stopped. No magic explanations there, not even from the fairy king.

Before they left, her mother barged into her room, now entirely in witch black which made the green face and hand paint even stranger. She pulled the earphones off Callie's head. "Well, we're off now. The candy's in the big tub at the door. We'll be at the Turners' house. I've put their number next to the phone."

Callie nodded, reaching for the earphones which her mother had tucked under one green arm.

"Now listen, Callie, if Nick is more than a minute or two late, I want you to call the Piatt house. Mrs. Piatt has never met a deadline in her life. And the kids are just like her. Honestly, I wish you didn't have this paper. I have a funny feeling . . ."

Her mother often had funny feelings. They never amounted to much.

Callie nodded again. "Deadline, phone number, funny feeling. I've got it! Let me get back to my article, Mom."

"How are you doing on it, sweetie?"

"It's a tough one."

"Well, journalism shouldn't be so tough. It's pretty straightforward, I thought. Just who-what-when-where-how."

"It's also *why*. At least the best journalism is," Callie said, quoting her teacher. "And it's the *why* I'm stuck on."

"Oh," her mother said, waving a dismissing and very green hand, "the *why* is easy, of course. Brass Rat just wants to make beautiful music." She handed the earphones back.

"Right." Callie took the earphones, which now sported green paint. She took a tissue and cleaned them. "The whole point of this stupid story is that Gringras and Brass Rat just want to make beautiful music. So they came to Noho the night before Halloween. How could I have been so dense as to miss that?"

"Now, now . . ." her mother said, "watch your tone. Remember I'm the witch. Not you!"

"Grab your broom, sweetie, time to rock and roll!" Her father's voice floated up the stairs.

Cackling loudly, her mother left.

Callie slammed the earphones back on, changed the CD, relieved to listen to the music of "Dante's Prayer" by Loreena McKennitt, relieved to be alone at last.

She wrote her story four separate times, and printed them out in different fonts, just for something to do. Each version sounded nuttier than the last: Rats. Pipers. Souls.

She tried to make connections between them. One was very science-fictional. One was straight Tolkien fantasy. One was clearly a fairy tale. The fourth was just plain nuts.

"I'll flunk journalism with this," she said aloud. "And I'll deserve to. Maybe I should just become a fiction writer. Maybe I should tell folk tales like Granny Kirkpatrick." She balled the stories up one after another until she had the four sitting by the side of her computer. "All they're good for is basketball." She quickly sank two in the wastebasket across the room.

Taking the headphones off, she ran her fingers through her hair to unflatten it. The house was quiet. Too quiet. She listened carefully, expecting to hear something from outside—cars pulling up to disgorge their costumed passengers, the shriek of kids trick-or-treating, doorbells ringing.

"Probably already gone by our street," she told herself, before putting the headphones on again.

Then she went on to AOL and tried to send instant messages to Josee and Alison, to tell them how awful the article was, and how sorry she was for acting so stupid to them in school, and what a hard time she was having. But neither of them was online.

"Of course, dummy," she told herself, smacking her forehead with the flat of her hand for real this time. "They're out trick-or-treating. Getting muchos chocolates. Having fun. Not thinking about me." Suddenly she was furious with herself for having volunteered to write the story.

Volunteered? She'd begged to do it. She'd shouldered the other students aside, practically trampled on them, to get the chance to write the stupid thing. And now . . .

Who cares about the dumb old band, anyway, she thought. *Or their exit-ential anthem. Or whatever Mars had called it. Who cares if they lost all their money or had to pay a teind or a blood guilt payment or whatever. And who flipping cares if rats dance all over them.*

She felt sorry for herself for about five minutes. And did a really good job of it, computing her midterm grade with a possible F and then a D and liking neither of the results. Changed back to the Clapton CD. The song about his dead kid helped her bad mood along.

Finally, she tore the earphones off and flung them across the room.

Enough! She was going to crack this story if it killed her. *And it just might!* she thought. *I'll just write what happened and leave the "why" of it to someone else.*

But try as she might, she couldn't write it in a straightforward, connect-the-dots manner. It seemed even weirder on the page that way. She couldn't see what the dancing rats and the blood guilt had to do with anything, so she deleted the story and put her head in her hands.

Maybe she needed to back into the stupid thing. Just let it rip. What her journalism teacher called "noodling," a word for going off on a controlled association.

"You mean 'Free association'?" John Grenzke had asked.

"Nothing free about it at all," the teacher had answered. "You've already paid your dues by doing your research. Like Watson on the double-decker bus suddenly coming up with the structure of DNA."

John had understood the reference, if nobody else had, nodding his head. He had that kind of mind. *Probably go to*

Harvard one day, Callie thought. *Not that he can write.*

She picked up a pen. "Okay—controlled association!" She scribbled the word *soul* on a Post-it note, then spelled it backwards and inside out: l-u-o-s, o-u-l-s, l-o-u-s.

"Louse indeed!" She grimaced. "Lousy anyway."

Then she spelled it s-o-l-e and pasted the Post-it on her computer.

"*Sole,* meaning alone, solo, one." She shook her head. "And I really am all alone and out there on this one."

She tried putting the word *sole* into a Google search, only her fingers slipped and she typed *soldo* instead.

A load of gibberish came up. She thought it might be Italian.

"All right, then," she whispered, "what's this when it's in English?"

The dictionary revealed that a "soldo" was a kind of Italian coin.

"So maybe . . ." she told herself slowly, "maybe I misunderstood. Maybe Alabas really said *Silver or gold or soldos.*"

She tried saying that quickly: *Silver or gold or soldos.* After ten times, she could almost believe *soldos* was what Alabas had actually been saying. It certainly made more sense than rats and pied pipers.

"I could call Mars again and ask him." But she knew he was busy with his frat party. Besides, she was mad at him, blowing her off that way. The white knight's armor was seriously tarnished.

"Time for a soda or a slice of cake or something." *Because,* she thought, *sugar will shock my system. Nothing like a good kick-start.*

AT THE FIRST LANDING ON the stairs, she passed the grandfather clock and saw it was already past nine.

"How did it get to be this late? Time sure flies . . ." Though she hadn't been having any fun.

It suddenly occurred to her that Nick had been due back at eight.

She couldn't believe he was a whole hour late. Usually he was such a goody-goody. Not like Mars, who'd never made a curfew in his life and had talked and smiled his way out of every punishment. But even if the Piatts couldn't read a clock face, Nicky was sure to have bugged them till they got him home on time.

"Oh, Nicky, you are in *big* trouble!" Though she knew she wouldn't rat on him.

Rats!

Again the scene of the dancing rodents came to mind. How they clapped their little paws, how they swayed to the music of the flute.

She shivered all the way into the kitchen.

15 · The Guardian and the Flower

Gringras remembered another clearing, deep in the Great Forest, far out in the eastern reaches of his father's kingdom, nearly into Unseelie territory. There grew a plant that flowered only once a century.

Gringras and Alabas had ridden hard and traveled far, managing to reach the clearing the day before the plant was due to bloom.

"It doesn't look like much does it?" remarked Alabas.

The plant shot straight up out of the ground to a height of two feet. Its stem was dull green with some darker splotches and it had two even duller, splotchier leaves on opposite sides.

"We shall see how it looks in the morning," Gringras replied. "For now we make camp."

They tied their horses to a nearby tree and pitched two small tents. Alabas made a small fire while Gringras played his flute softly. Soon, two rabbits wandered into the clearing and sat in front of the piper.

"Rabbit? I thought we could have a grander meal with the

completion of our quest so near at hand." Alabas had sounded disappointed.

Gringras dropped his flute and snatched up the rabbits—a buck and a doe, their little eyes showing no fear.

"I dare not risk any larger enchantments this close to the Unseelie lands. To do so might provoke the final war between our kingdoms."

Alabas nodded and they cooked their dinner in silence.

Knowing what a superb hostage any prince of the Seelie Court would make—even a middle one—they set their wards that evening with extra care. When they finally slept, it was in fits and starts.

In the morning, they woke and saw the plant had flowered overnight. The once small, dull, stick was now man-high and covered with glowing pink flowers.

"Gaudy thing," Alabas noted, "Let's pluck it and head home."

Without reply, Gringras strode purposely to his horse. He began rummaging through his saddlebags before speaking.

"I may have forgotten to mention a few things, Alabas."

"Yes? What did you forget to mention?" Off in the distance there came a loud thud. "And what was that noise?"

Having found what he was looking for, Gringras grunted in satisfaction and pulled a leather glove from his saddlebag.

"I mentioned the flower blooms once a century, correct?"

"Yes."

There was another thud.

"I told you that it causes anyone who eats it to fall into a state indistinguishable from death for a period of three days?"

"Yes."

There was another thud closer by.

"I explained to you the virtues of this plant as a poison: odorless, tasteless, leaves no trace?"

"Again, yes."

The thuds were coming quicker and closer. The horses began whinnying, their eyes rolled back in terror, showing the whites.

"I recall saying that the journey was arduous and the location next to Unseelie territory dangerous." Gringras pulled the glove onto his right hand and deftly untied his horse from its tree. He slapped it on its flank and it galloped into the woods. He nodded at Alabas.

With a quick glance over his shoulder to where the thuds were coming from, Alabas scampered to his horse and began working the knot.

Meanwhile, Gringras marched to the middle of the clearing and rolled his head back and forth, loosening up.

"What I may have forgotten to mention," Gringras said, pulling his long sword from the ornate scabbard at his hip, "is that the flower has a guardian."

The knot came free in Alabas' hand and his horse bolted straight across the clearing past Gringras.

"A very large guardian," Gringras added.

Just then, a huge bear-like creature burst into the clearing opposite the two men. It was house-high and covered in a dark, mossy fur. Roaring, it reared up on its hind legs as Alabas' horse skidded to a halt in front of it. The poor mount seemed ready to expire from fright. The guardian scooped it up in a huge taloned claw.

"What are you waiting for, Gringras?" Alabas screamed. "Blast it with a spell! This is no time to worry about alerting the Unseelie Court."

The guardian's face split nearly in half, revealing razor-sharp teeth, three feet long.

"And one thing I am certain I did not mention . . ." Gringras spoke calmly as the creature popped the screaming horse into its mouth whole, "is that the guardian is immune to magic."

Sighing, Alabas pulled two long knives from twin sheaths at the small of his back. "You did indeed leave out a few details, my lord."

Gringras stood firm and faced the beast, long sword in hand as befitted a prince of Faerie. Even a middle prince. Meanwhile, Alabas circled around behind it with his knives, as befitted someone who wanted to live for at least another hour or two.

The guardian charged. It was quick for its size but Gringras was quicker, dashing to the side to avoid the deadly claws and swinging his weapon in a sweeping arc that ended with a meaty thwock! in the back of the guardian's left leg. He dove and rolled as the guardian turned, springing up behind it once more to deliver another solid blow to the other leg. This time the guardian was faster. It spun on its wounded legs and caught Gringras a ringing blow with its claw.

The prince went flying, landing on his back, dazed, and the guardian roared in triumph as it dove forward for the kill.

Through blurry eyes, Gringras saw Alabas leap high into the air and come down on the guardian's back, burying both his knives to the hilt in its neck. The creature let out one final growl and Alabas rode it, dying, to the ground.

Alabas addressed Gringras who was rising slowly, shaking his head to clear it.

"Anything else you forgot to mention?"

"I believe that is all."

Alabas recovered his knives and deftly snipped a flower from the century plant. "Let's go home then." He grinned, adding, "My lord."

An Unseelie horn sounded in the far distance and they ran from the clearing, following the tracks of Gringras' horse.

16 · Missing

The Piatts' number was on the bulletin board in large red letters. Callie grabbed a cookie from the big jar by the oven. Chocolate chip, fresh baked. How could she resist?

Then she went over to the phone. Picking it up, she was about to dial when some flashing blue lights outside caught her eye. She glanced out the kitchen window.

A police car was parked in front of their driveway, and behind it a second car.

She slammed down the phone, her heart beating double-time.

Why are the police here?

She ran to the front door and threw it open, and ran outside.

Something has happened to Nicky! she thought frantically. *Or Mars. Or Mom.* She bit her lip. *Or Dad.*

Her parents' car screeched into the driveway, almost colliding with the police car. Before it could come to a full stop, her mother leaped out, her witch hat askew and her black robe billowing behind her. She ran to Callie and grabbed her up tight, nearly smothering her.

"Nicky," she cried. "Is Nicky home?"

"No, Mom, I'm sorry, I lost track of time and . . ."

"No!" her mother screamed and then her father was there, too, enveloping both of them in his big arms. Callie looked up into his eyes and saw they glistened with tears.

Oh God, something has *happened to Nicky—and it's all my fault!*

A short policewoman with a face the color of leaf mold cleared her throat. "Folks, there's no time for a family re-union. . . ." Realizing how harsh that sounded, she started over. "Folks, I'm dreadfully sorry, but we need to talk to your daughter. You told us she was probably at home, and luckily you were right. But as she's the only child in the neighborhood who doesn't seem to have gone missing to-night, we need to ask her some questions."

Her partner, who'd been silent until now, turned to Callie's father. "Now," he said shortly.

Callie was stunned and pulled back from her parents. *The only child in the neighborhood not missing? What about Josee and Alison? Or the Napier kids she sat for—Mollie and Kaitlin and Sean? What about the triplets down the block? Or little Jodie Ryan in her wheelchair? What about the Piatts?* But she didn't name them aloud. She couldn't.

Then she thought wildly: *If only I'd written the story sooner, if only Mars had talked to me, if only I'd told Mom and Dad the crazy things I suspected.*

"My . . . fault . . ." she sobbed.

Her mother held her tight, saying into her hair, "Not

your fault, Callie. Not yours. The Turners' grandchildren were due back at 8:30. Their parents called the party where we were to say they weren't home yet and asked what to do. Then everyone at the party got on cell phones. In minutes we knew the worst. All the children in the neighborhood seemed to be gone. *All* gone. When we couldn't get hold of you, we thought you were missing, too, though Daddy thought you might have your headphones on and hadn't heard the phone."

"I didn't, I didn't hear," Callie said, not knowing if she should feel guilty or relieved. *God,* she thought, *I'll never be able to listen to Eric Clapton or Loreena McKennitt again.*

Gray-faced, her father added, "It's like a terrorist plot or something. I can't wrap my mind around it." He gave her another hug. "Thank God you didn't go trick-or-treating, Callie. If you were *both* gone . . ."

Callie saw that fear and sorrow had already changed her father's face. The eyes were drawn down in a way she'd never seen before. His lower lip was trembling. She looked up at her mother who was silently crying green tears. "We have to call Mars."

"We already have," her father said, wiping his nose on his wizard's cloak sleeve. "We had to know we had one child left."

"You thought *I* was missing, too? And you *cared*?" Being a middle kid, even the middle with seven years on either side, did sometimes make you wonder. Being hemmed in and sewn up tight all the time made you wonder even more. Not loved, but owned. Not cared about but cared for.

"Care? Of course we care, Calcephony. How could you

think otherwise?" her father asked. "We love you. We love you tremendously."

Callie could feel his arms around her trembling. She'd never known her father to tremble. It scared her.

The policewoman cleared her throat. "Folks, we really need to speak to your daughter. Time is of the essence here. If she knows anything . . ."

"How could I know anything?" Callie said, more loudly than she meant. "I was upstairs in my room." But it wasn't entirely true that she knew nothing. She knew about the band. About the rats. Still, she hesitated, realizing how weird that would sound. *No,* she thought, *not weird—stark, raving loony.*

The policewoman looked at her oddly. "What is it?"

Callie thought, *My face must be broadcasting my thoughts.* "It's nothing. . . ."

Putting a leaf-mold hand on Callie's, the policewoman spoke quietly but intensely to her, never taking her eyes away from Callie's eyes. "Anything you can tell us, no matter how small, how silly, how . . ."

"How crazy?" Callie asked.

"Not even how *crazy* . . ." the policewoman assured her.

Knowing that there was really only one way all of the facts hung together, even though it sounded like a fairy tale, a horror story, actually, Callie grabbed a deep breath, then plunged ahead. "I think I *do* know what's happening."

"Kidnappers?" Her mother's voice broke on the final syllable. "But we don't have much money."

"Terrorists," her dad said. "I'm sure of it."

"Tell me," the policewoman demanded.

"Now!" her partner added, as if that were the only word he knew.

Callie nodded. "Well, it has to do with rock and roll and . . ."

"Drugs!" the policeman said. A second word, just as loud.

"No, no, not drugs." Callie held up her hand. "Geez, officer—these are little kids. Trick-or-treaters."

The policeman nodded, if a bit reluctantly.

"It has to do," Callie said slowly, "with the Pied Piper of Hamelin and rats."

The policeman made a face and turned to his partner. "What's she talking about? She on something?"

"On *to* something," Callie insisted. "Something I discovered at the Brass Rat concert."

"Ratter, ratter, mad as a hatter," her mom began to sing.

"It's the shock, that's what it is," her father said, putting an arm around each of them.

Callie looked up at him, willing him to understand. "Well, of course we're shocked, Dad. But that's not what I mean. The thing is—the Pied Piper of Hamelin is *here.* He's come around again. Really! I know this because of the dancing rats."

Tears starting down her green cheeks again, her mother began reciting, " 'Rats! They fought the dogs and killed the cats, and bit the babies in the cradles, and ate the cheeses out of the . . .' "

The policeman turned to his partner. "Is the whole family nuts?"

"Hank, let me deal with this," she told him and put her hand out to Callie. "Miss McCallan, we understand that this whole thing is a shock. It's a shock to us, too. But if you have any *real* information, we need to hear it."

"Wait," Callie said. "I have something to show you. It's in my room. I'll get it. It explains better than I can." She turned and ran back into the house. She could hear them following, but slowly, and arguing about how crazy she was and whether, in fact, she was trying to outrun or outwit them.

Taking the steps two at a time, she raced upstairs. At the landing, the clock seemed to shout at her: 9:50. The long hallway was dark, uninviting. She didn't stop to worry about it the way she sometimes did, but went straight to her bedroom at the very end of the hall.

She didn't remember having turned off the light, but her room was now badly lit only by the flickering of the computer screen. Picking up the two remaining balled–up articles from her desk, she ran back out. She figured she'd get the policewoman to read what she'd written, out loud, and then they'd all understand.

As she went down the hall past Nicky's room, she heard something familiar playing on his CD player. Funny that she hadn't heard it before. But it was as if all her senses were now on full alert. She slowed, took a step inside his room, then realized that what she was hearing was Brass Rat's latest CD, the one Nick had gotten at the concert. It was evidently on a continuous loop. The tune was the very one Gringras had been piping to the rats.

"It all comes back to rats!" she said in a hoarse whisper and burst into tears, because guilt had come flooding back as she stood in Nicky's room. If she'd gone out trick-or-treating with him, maybe he wouldn't be missing now.

Or maybe, her treacherous mind reminded her, *you'd be missing with him.*

The flute was mesmerizing and for a long moment she stood still, staring at the blinking light on the CD player. Then she came to, slammed her hand down on the black plastic, turning the player off. The blinking light disappeared, but somehow the song kept going on, a twisting, twining sound that seemed to bind her, to call her, to summon her to follow.

The music made her turn from the player and look at the window. Stuffing one of the paper balls in her pocket, she dropped the other on the the CD player where it rolled off on to the floor. She ignored it and tugged at the window till it opened, then climbed out onto the little balcony where she and Nick had often had tea parties when they were both younger.

There was a soft wind puzzling through the trees. For late October it seemed very warm. The moon was full and orange. She knew in the back part of her mind that her parents and the police were coming up the stairs. Probably talking about her erratic behavior, her smart talk. Arguing about the puzzle of the missing trick-or-treaters. Her mother was probably crying. Maybe sobbing. Her father might still be trembling. The cops were surely flinging accusations.

But that didn't seem to matter now. Oddly, all that mattered was the song. The haunting flute that was calling to her.

She took a deep breath and the air both burned and soothed her throat at the same time.

"Nicky," she whispered. "Hold on, Bugbrain. I'm coming."

She was determined to bring him back. She believed that

finding him was the least she could do, having failed to go with him or keep track of the time. But her head was muzzy with the flute song now, and she wasn't thinking straight. She reached over, touched the trellis which was still covered with late blooming bloodred roses, swung her leg over the railing of the balcony, and started to clamber down.

She never felt the thorns.

Skirting the empty police car, she didn't notice the light in her bedroom window where her parents and the two cops were opening closets and looking under the bed, her mother crying and her father on his cell phone calling Mars again. Or the lights in the Temples' house next door where people were watching the television, frantic for news. Or the dog on Mrs. Lee's front porch whining but afraid to go down the steps.

Instead, she got to the road and began to dance.

One foot, two, glide and glide, she followed the song of the flute along Elm Street, heading toward Main Street, the piping luring her on and on and on.

17 · A Death in the Family

Flute in hand, Gringras remembered more: he remembered the quiet dinner with his older brother, Tormalas the heir. He remembered letting his brother prattle on about politics and the possibility of war with the Unseelie Court. Meanwhile in the kitchen, Alabas poisoned the food. Poisoned Gringras' food.

Tormalas' tasters had eaten heartily off the heir's plate, pronouncing it safe. After that it was a simple matter for the switch to be made. A little misdirection ("Look out!"), a little sleight of hand (Gringras dabbled in the more mundane illusions as well as the true magic), and soon Tormalas was chewing happily on venison chops lightly seasoned with century plant.

He ate for three more minutes and then slumped to the floor, to all appearances stone-dead. Appearances, as Gringras knew and had planned for, could be deceiving. And nowhere was this truer than in Faerie.

THE HEIR'S BODY LAY IN *state for three days.*

On the first day, the attendants washed and dressed the dead prince in his funeral attire of white and gold. They set his body in a bier decorated with wild peonies and cultivated roses. The family gathered in a mourning circle around the coffin.

King Merrias, a stoic figure, sat still from dawn till dusk, while his wife wept impressively and tore at her long silver hair.

Gringras tried to look suitably melancholy. He kept dabbing at his eyes with an enormous white handkerchief. Occasionally he let out a large sigh.

Wynn, the youngest, had been sent for, but had not yet returned from whatever adventure he was currently on. Gringras had counted on that.

On the second day, the antechamber where Tormalas lay was opened to the public. Creatures from afar came to pay their respects. Fey lords and ladies in gaudy, shimmering raiment strode majestically by the body, barely deigning to glance down. Small brownies and hearth witches clucked their tongues as they passed, sighing at the waste of it all. Phookas, selkies, and other shape-shifters padded, hopped, or slithered by. Pixies and winged fairies wafted over the open coffin and wept beautifully, their translucent wings fluttering self-consciously. Even a lone boggart—emissary from the Unseelie Court—shambled past the coffin, glaring at it, perhaps angry he hadn't the chance to kill the prince himself.

Gringras watched the display with amusement, but was careful to show nothing on his face but the expected grief.

Wynn had still not arrived.

Custom and religion dictated that on the third day the body was moved outside and placed on a large wooden pyre, scheduled to be burned at midnight. A crowd gathered early, jostling for position around the tower. The faerie rulers were long-lived and a state funeral was a once-in-a-millennium event.

Gringras stood in the hall outside the throne room, waiting for an audience with his father that would confirm him as the new heir. He knew that, once he was confirmed—even after Tormalas' miraculous recovery, which should be happening a little after sunset—nothing short of Gringras' own death could remove the mantle of power from his shoulders.

A stentorian voice echoed from inside the king's audience chamber.

"Come." It was the High Chamberlain.

Gringras straightened his cloak and, running first one nervous hand through his hair and then the other, opened the door.

His father was not alone. At the king's side sat a handsome young man, broad of shoulder and strong of arm, with curly blonde locks crowning a pleasant, honest face. He was still dressed in his traveling clothes and, even though it was apparent he had rushed right to this chamber immediately after dismounting, he somehow managed to look fresh, clean, alert, and capable.

Wynn had finally come home.

18 · Music Man

Elm Street was quiet, as still as if it were some sort of painted backdrop to Callie's dance. Even the wind had stopped. No cars purred along the blacktop. No leaves fluttered down from the maples and oaks. No cats prowled the side streets. The traffic lights had for some unknown reason all gone dark. The world was lit spookily by the Halloween moon.

Yet there was one sound Callie could hear clearly, and that was the flute tune that pulled her along. That sound was so real, so palpable, she believed she could have put her hand on it and it would have felt like a rope.

She danced along Elm Street noticing and yet not noticing, the way one does in a dream. One step, two, glide and glide.

As she danced by Greene Hall, where the concert had been held the night before, she suddenly heard another bit of music. The same tune, but a different voice. It seemed to cut through the golden rope that bound her by a single strand.

Still dancing—one step, two, glide and glide—she hesitated a moment to listen more carefully. That hesitation wasn't willed, it just sort of happened.

This new voice was lower, sweeter, less insistent. She tried to think what it could be. It didn't have the breathiness of the flute. The sound seemed more sustained, yet at the same time less fluid. There were occasional chords. Something strummed.

And then, all at once, she realized she was hearing a guitar. *Guitar!*

She stopped in her tracks.

Scott played the guitar. Beautiful Scott with the wide Viking face, the long golden braid, and the deep ocean blue eyes. Who was sixteen going on forty. Her crush from what seemed years and miles ago, though it was just twenty-four hours away.

Looking over to the steps of John M. Greene Hall, she saw Scott haloed in the moonlight, hunched over his guitar and playing with such intensity, she thought she would cry. The sound he made was brilliant, clear, beautiful, and much more innocent than the sensuous piping of the flute.

"Scott," she whispered, his name another kind of song, but he didn't hear her.

The notes of the guitar drew her to him, one step, two, glide and glide. And the flute's binding power was suddenly cut through, as if by a knife.

She danced quietly to the foot of the steps and stopped, watching him play, afraid to break the spell of his music, afraid to call attention to herself, afraid that if she spoke the flute would find her again.

Minute after minute she watched his right hand pick out tunes, strands of pearls on the strings. Minute after minute she watched his left hand crawling up and down the neck of the guitar, marking the notes with precise fingering. But he must have sensed her standing there, for finally he glanced up, his face momentarily innocent of all knowledge but his music. Then his face seemed to clear, as if he'd suddenly wakened.

"Hey . . ." he said, and stopped playing.

"Hey . . ." she replied.

He was no longer wearing the pants with the painted rats, but a pair of plain black jeans, and a leather jacket over a white tee. His hair was hanging loose, Alice in Wonderland style, down on his shoulders.

Briefly she wondered what she had on, hoped it was better than her soccer shirt and Old Navy jeans, knew it wasn't, and houghed through her nose like a horse.

"You been here long?" he asked.

"Long enough," she said.

"It's sure quiet in this town," he said, then ran his fingers along the guitar's neck, just playing a scale, but the notes shivered up and down Callie's spine as if his hand had wandered there by mistake.

"*Too* quiet," Callie responded. She tried to say more, but it was as if her tongue was stuck to the roof of her mouth. Never at a loss for words, she was wordless now. She tried once more, forcing out the first word: "Rats!" And then it all came out in a rush. She told him everything: the missing trick-or-treaters, Gringras on the fire escape, the dancing rats. She even told him, though she blushed in the telling, what she'd overheard.

He put down his guitar, laying it carefully on its back on the step beside him. His hand hesitated for a moment over the instrument, as though he were comforting it, calming it. When he looked up at her again, his face seemed strange, pained, as if she'd just stuck a dagger into his heart. Then he sighed, and as though attuned to his every utterance, the guitar echoed the sigh back.

"So, it's true," he whispered. Callie had to lean far in to hear him.

She realized that he wanted her to ask. So she did. "What's true?"

"For years . . ." he began. Stopped, took a deep breath, and started again. "For years I've worked hard at *not* understanding. 'Just play the music, man,' I told myself. Because the music is all that matters. The song that has to be played. Not how we get paid or how much. Not what the venue, where the gig. Not even the audience. Long as I've got enough for food and some new leathers and my picks and strings, as long as I've got gas for the bike . . ." He nodded at the motorcycle parked near the bottom step which Callie hadn't even noticed before. "As long as I've got that, I'm fine, man." He sighed again and once more the guitar sounded like wind stroking across the strings. Callie saw that in the moonlight, his blue eyes looked faded, ghostly, the skin of his cheeks almost translucent, like rare glass.

"But this time it's different?"

He nodded. "*Silver or gold or souls,*" he said. And I thought that was okay. Because it's always been silver or gold. Every seven years. Like clockwork, man. I never asked what Gringras meant by 'souls.' I thought it was a joke. He jokes a lot, you know. And I don't understand half of what he's gassing on about. But it never seemed to matter much. At least to me. The music's been *that* good."

She sighed back and all the while her head thought, *I've never been a sigher. A fairy tale type. I'm a hardheaded journalist.* But she sighed nonetheless. Because she wasn't a journalist, not yet. She was only fourteen years old and in high school.

"But it matters now," she whispered.

"Because it's children," Scott said. There was a powerful cry in what he said.

"Then you believe me?"

He nodded. "Yes, I believe you. Because it all fits. Silver or gold or souls. Not a joke. Not a joke at all. And I can't let that happen. Not to kids." He shivered. "Kids—I don't know a lot about them. Except I can't let it happen."

"*We* can't let it happen," Callie whispered, daring to put them together. Then she added, *"Again."*

"Again?"

She sighed again, mostly at what she now had to say. "I tried to write about it for my school paper, before the kids in the neighborhood disappeared, but it seemed too far out, like I was trying to force the puzzle pieces to fit. But now they all slide into place." She held up her hand and counted on her fingers. "Hamelin. The Children's Crusade. The little princes in the tower. All the other places kids have disappeared and were never found. He's a regular milk carton creep."

Scott leaned over, picked up his guitar, and stood. "Not on my watch." He sounded like a soldier. "My dad took me from my mom. Moved us away across the country. Gave me a new name. I don't even know my old one. I never saw her again."

"You could still find her," Callie offered, thinking all the while: *I'm talking to Scott. Really talking.* "After this, I mean. You could find her." She hesitated, then added, "I could help. There's computer searches and stuff."

He shook his head, and the golden hair shimmered. "She'd be . . ." He hesitated. "Awfully old now. Maybe even dead."

"Not much older than my mom and dad," Callie said. "Couldn't be."

"You don't know," he said, started to say more, and stopped himself. "You couldn't possibly believe it anyway."

"Try me," she whispered.

But as if he hadn't heard, he said, "It's the children who count now. Not me and my old problems. So, reporter girl—"

"Callie," she said. "Callie McCallan." She wondered if she should say more. Like where she lived. Or how old she was.

"Callie, put this on your back." He handed her the guitar and she grabbed it with a kind of reverence. "We'll take the bike. It'll be faster."

"Faster to *where?*" Then she suddenly remembered—to where Nicky and the other kids were. How could she have forgotten?

But her question seemed to stop him cold. "Damned if I know," he replied.

The minute he said that, she heard the flute again. It was

less compelling this time because she was standing so close to Scott, but there was no mistaking it.

"Do you hear that?" she asked.

He nodded and held out his hand. "If we find the flute . . ."

She nodded back. "We find the kids."

Without hesitation, she took his hand and followed him to the motorcycle, a black Harley Electra Glide.

"The Classic," he said, fishing two helmets out of the backpack and handing one to her.

The helmet fitted her head as if designed for her.

Then Scott climbed on the bike and Callie, like a princess out of the old stories, got on behind. Putting her arms around his waist, she held tight, her head cheek down against his leather jacket. It smelled of many winds and many streets. It smelled of Scott. She made herself forget about all the girls before her who must have ridden with him.

"Which way?" he asked over his shoulder.

At first she had a hard time hearing with the helmet on, but she strained to listen for a minute. Finally she heard the flute song, as if it were being piped into the helmet, and she pointed down the hill toward the center of town.

He kicked the bike into gear and the motor caught.

For a moment the flute song was hidden.

For a moment Callie despaired.

But once they were out on Elm, going down the hill, Callie heard the flute again.

"That way!" she called out, pointing over Scott's shoulder at every turning. "Now that way!"

So street by street, she guided them along till they crossed the bridge spanning the Connecticut and the turning onto Route 47.

"There!" Callie said, and they headed along the winding road toward the little mountain range ringing the foot of the Valley.

19 · Resurrection

Gringras' casting was nearly at an end. As he tied the loose ends of his spell with notes both sung and played, he remembered the words his father had spoken on the day Tormalas's body was to be burned.

"I thought you should both hear this together." King Merrias had stood and motioned Gringras to an empty chair by Wynn's side.

Gringras would have preferred standing but the old man had stared silently at him until he took his seat.

Then the king began to pace the long crimson carpet. "I have given much thought to my choice. Balancing precedence. And this is what I have decided. We are nearly at war. The Unseelie test our borders daily. If I die in battle, Faerie will need a warrior to lead it." He looked pointedly at Gringras. "Not a musician."

Not a musician? *thought Gringras frantically.* But I am next in line! *"Respectfully, sir, but tradition . . ."*

"Tradition favors the oldest living son—it does not require

it." The king looked almost pained as he made his proclama-tion. "Gringras, I am sorry. You are a fine young man. Charm-ing. Intelligent. Talented."

Talented. *Gringras wanted to spit on the palace floor.*

"But I have made Wynn heir to the throne," *the king contin-ued.* "It is for the good of Faerie, you understand."

Gringras could not speak. He could not breathe. Tormalas was sure to know who was at fault when he recovered. Gringras knew his only protection from his brother's wrath was to have been his position as heir. Without that he was ruined. Because his father was right. He was no warrior compared to either of his brothers. Just fine, charming, intelligent. Talented.

And ruined.

Ruined. Like a cracked pillar thrown down in the wood.

He almost smiled. Thinking of lyrics at a time like this!

Wynne looked at him with honest compassion.

If you only knew, *Gringras screamed at him silently before stumbling silently and dramatically out the throne room door.*

I need air. I need room to think. *Perhaps he could go back in time and undo this disaster. Surely there was a spell for that. He looked down at his ring, hopefully.*

Reaching the castle's main door, he threw it open. The sun was just lowering in a blaze of red and yellow and Tormalas' pyre was silhouetted against the bloody sky. Suddenly, all of Gringras' fears and regret turned to anger. He no longer cared what happened to him; he needed to punish someone for his misfortunes. And Tormalas was a handy and helpless target.

He marched straight for the thirty-foot tower, on top of which lay his brother's funeral pyre. Spectators and mourners crowded the square. Brownies, red caps, boogies, and peris, who in life never associated, now stood elbow to elbow waiting for the spectacle of the prince's funeral fire.

Ignoring their disapproving stares, Gringras bulled his way through. As he edged closer to the pyre, the way became too crowded for mere physical blows to clear it. Thrusting his hand forward, ring outward, Gringras uttered a word of power. A blast of wind threw aside any creatures in his path.

Mounting the steps three at a time, he came to the bier where his brother lay. Drawing out his sword, Gringras lifted it high over his head two-handed. The crowd gasped and the door to the castle burst open once more, this time spewing forth Alabas, the king, and the new heir, all running toward the pyre.

"Gringras!" Alabas shouted. "It's over!"

The sun finally dipped below the horizon. Gringras turned, sword still raised, and looked back toward the castle. The courtyard was lit now by faerie fires in four corners, the magical glow washing the color from faces, making the onlookers look as dead as Tormalas.

Alabas spoke once more, softly, for now he was on the tower, too, close enough to touch Gringras, though even he knew better than to dare any such thing. "Don't add murder to our crimes."

Our crimes, repeated Gringras to himself. It was that phrase that finally stopped him. Whatever happened now, at least he would share it with one other. The other conspirator. His one true friend.

The anger drained from him and he lowered his sword.

The sun set.

Tormalas sat up.

20 · Trail of Sweets

For a long while Callie buried her face in Scott's leather jacket, shutting out the Halloween dark. That way she could concentrate on sounds: the high temptations of the flute, the ground bass of the motorcycle, the moaning of the wind as it whistled past her ears.

When Scott suddenly slowed the bike to a stop and cut the engine, she looked up, startled.

"Why have we . . ."

He pointed to the roadside. "Look."

"I don't see anything."

He got off and—after a minute—she did, too.

"Give me my guitar," he said, stabilizing the bike with its kickstand, then holding out his hand.

She swung the guitar off her back and gave it to him.

He strummed his fingers across the strings. The sound seemed to light up the roadside, because suddenly Callie saw what he saw. There were four discarded wizards' hats, a set of Velcroed fairy wings, and seven light-saber wands.

Dozens of plastic orange jack-o'-lanterns filled with candy lay on their sides, scattering Hershey bars and lollipops, candy kisses and Baby Ruths, candy corn and Almond Joys on the grassy verge.

"It looks like a Halloween graveyard," she burst out, not meaning to be funny, yet both of them broke into nervous laughter at her observation. The laughter was liberating, and not just because it exorcised some of the dread of the night. It also seemed to have cut through the incessant piping of the flute.

Scott stopped laughing first. Kneeling down by the discarded costumes, he stroked the silken inlay of the fairy wings with his right hand, his expression somewhere between anger and relief.

"How did you see these things?" Callie asked.

He paused as if considering. "I guess I've been with Gringras and his music too long."

She nodded. That made a kind of sense. "So how come I didn't?"

"Glamour."

She looked puzzled. "What do you mean, *glamour?* Like Hollywood? That kind of glamour?"

He shook his head slowly, then stood up and, turning toward her, started singing one of the songs from the concert the night before. Not full out, as if in performance, but in a strange, whispery voice which made it even more powerful. She hadn't caught all the lyrics when they'd played at Greene Hall, surrounded as they'd been, drowned by the hard-driving guitar, the bass, the heavy drums. But now she understood every single word.

"I put the glamour on this space,
  Transforming every human face,
  And leaving nothing left to trace
  When morning finally comes.

"I put the magic on this spot
  So what you see and think you've got,
  And what you fear is what is not,
  When morning finally comes.

  "When morning comes
    The mundane morn
    When magic is
    No longer worn.

  "When morning comes
    The killer dawn
    When spells are done
    And magic gone.

"So stand upon my sacred ground
  For what you hold's not what you've found,
  And to this glamour you'll be bound
  When morning finally comes."

"That kind of glamour," Scott added.

"I still don't get it." In the moonlight Callie's face was creased with doubt.

"Magic. Enchantment. Putting a glamour on something or someone means to change it by magic, alter it in some subtle way so it's no longer what it once was. At least that's what Gringras says it means. What Alabas says about it, I can't tell you."

Callie put her hands on her hips. "I'm fourteen, you know. In high school. Don't condescend to me." Suddenly she hated him, wondered what she was doing out at night, here, with a stranger. Suddenly worried that all the things her parents had been guarding her against might come true, here, by the mountain. With a guy who wasn't exactly the sixteen he seemed to be.

"I mean, I can't tell you because I don't actually know. And Alabas doesn't talk much. When he does, it's often in some old language the two of them speak together," he said. "I only know a few of the words—*teind* and *byre* and . . ."

"*Breeks* and *gyre?*" She remembered the curse that Alabas had called down on the manager's head. "Is it magic? Some of it sounds like my Scottish grandmother talking." She suddenly remembered something Alison had said. "And some comes from an old folk song."

He shrugged. "Beats me. *Breeks* means pants and *gyre* a kind of . . . of turning thing." For a moment, his hand looked like it was stirring some sort of batter. "Like a whirlwind."

"Pants and a whirlwind? Now that *really* doesn't make any sense." But she smiled to take away the sting of what she was saying.

He didn't smile back. Instead he turned, and in an attitude of listening, stared across the street toward Mt. Holyoke, the small mountain in the center of the range.

Callie imitated him, but she couldn't hear anything. So

she took off her helmet, holding it by the strap, and tried again.

Silence.

No wind. No road sounds. No birds. No flute. The unnaturalness of it made her shiver. Again, she thought of her parents.

Wanting to get Scott talking again, if only to cut through the eerie quiet, she said, "So you think the reason I didn't see this stuff—this trail of Halloween sweets and hats and wings and all—was that it had a glamour on it? An enchantment?"

The moonlight cast his hair in silver, yet still he looked no more than sixteen years old.

"Right."

"So the police wouldn't have seen anything either."

He nodded, leaning forward as if paying attention to something else, something beyond her ken.

"Scott, look at me."

He didn't move, only leaned even further into whatever it was that had caught his attention.

"Please." She hated the whine in her voice. Controlled it. Spoke again, this time without the whine, but in a whisper. "Please."

Slowly he turned back.

"What are you doing?"

"Listening to the flute."

"But it's gone."

"No, it's not. Not entirely."

Once again she listened hard, heard nothing. "Yes it . . ."

He picked up her hand and put it on the strings of his guitar. She could feel them vibrate under her palm. The vibration traveled along the top of her skin, all the way up her arm, along her neck, and curled up and into her ear.

It was as if a layer of that dreadful silence had been peeled away. As if she'd been asleep before and was now suddenly totally awake.

The flute was singing. Only this time she heard it plain, without its glamour, without its sensuous beckoning. Now the tune was a darker, more sinister sound, the kind of music that—in a movie—would have warned that the monster was near. For a moment she hesitated, shivering. Then she pointed to the sign that said **SKINNER STATE PARK**.

"That way." Toward the road that wound around the volcanic rock, and to the Summit House, the big white building that perched like an eagle's nest at the very top.

"Don't be scared," Scott said, but his voice trembled a bit.

"I'm not scared," Callie lied.

She put on the helmet and Scott got back on the motorcycle. Jamming down with his foot to start the bike, he held out a hand to Callie. She climbed up behind him again and they headed on to the winding road. There they climbed steadily beneath overlaced branches of maple, oak, and pine, black against the moon-lightened sky.

All the way up, Callie was thinking: *This is wrong. This is a bad idea. Mom and Dad are right.* Her head kept sending her warnings: *Turn around. Go home.* But they kept on going, because it was, after all, the only thing they could do. The only way they could find Gringras. And Nicky. And the children. And all the answers.

Every now and then, when she lost the thread of the flute song, Callie put her hand over her shoulder and touched the strings of Scott's guitar. Each time the music would travel up her arm, across her shoulder, up her neck, and into her ear, calling to that other music.

Ahead, always ahead.

The flute and its master were up at the top. And where Gringras was, Callie knew the children would be, too.

What she didn't know was whether any of them were still alive.

21 - Reunion

Tormalas had looked up quizzically and Gringras shrugged, sheathing his sword. Then offering his left hand, Gringras spoke, his voice calm though his stomach was roiling. "Welcome back to the land of the living, Brother."

Tormalas said nothing but took in the entire scene: the pyre, the crowd, Alabas, his brother's so-recently sheathed sword. He remembered having dinner with Gringras and then nothing more. Tormalas had been trained since childhood to be a master politician, a nimble thinker. Gringras could see him putting it all together.

"I assume it has been three days," Tormalas said, taking the proffered hand.

Gringras nodded and pulled Tormalas to his feet. He was half a head taller than the younger prince.

"Father does not suspect you?"

Gringras shook his head, shrugged.

"He always had a blind spot where you were concerned." Tormalas stated this as fact. There was no blame in his voice.

"He passed me over." *They could have been talking about a dinner menu or a planned ball.*

Alabas cleared his throat, but they ignored him.

For a long moment, Tormalas considered his younger brother with a kind of seasoned affection before saying, "Then you are not the heir, which means it is treason you committed."

Gringras grinned defiantly. "It would not have been if it had worked."

Tormalas chuckled. "That *is debatable, Gringras. And that kind of thinking is why I am to be king, not you."*

Gringras laughed. "Neither me nor you, Brother. Father has chosen Wynn now."

Momentarily disconcerted, Tormalas was silent. Then he put his right hand on Gringras' shoulder and, bending a little, stared into his eyes, searching them. "I can find precedence to overturn that decision. Wynn will do my bidding. He always has. But you, Gringras—you I can no longer trust. I may have to see you hang."

"Well, if you see me hang," Gringras replied, *"it will be through just one eye."*

Before Tormalas could ask him what he meant, or Alabas could stop him, Gringras lashed out, intending merely to black his brother's eye. It was one last defiant act, one salve to his wounded pride. But, as luck would have it, Tormalas—who was well trained in the warrior's art—ducked to one side. Instead of hitting him in the eye, Gringras punched Tormalas square in the temple. His signet ring, sorcerously forged and full of powerful magicks, connected with the soft spot on Tormalas' skull.

Already weakened from three days near death, and suddenly

suffering a savage and unexpected blow that was both physical and magical, Tormalas collapsed backwards. He fell off the pyre and hit the ground thirty feet below.

This time he was, in fact, stone-dead. Both dead and, as the magic willed it, stone as well.

22 · Trail of Tears

The higher they went, the louder the flute got. On a final turn, Callie saw the park gates ahead of them with the empty parking lot looking like a dark cave.

"How could they have gotten this far without cars?" Callie asked. But her heart answered her. *Magic. Black and wicked.* And suddenly, it wasn't just that her mom and dad were right, but that Granny Kirkpatrick was right, too. *I should have paid more attention to her stories,* Callie thought.

Scott eased the bike into the darkness, turning off the lights and the engine. "Stay close," he said unnecessarily, holding out his hand.

Callie took it like a lifeline. His hand was cold in hers.

She pointed ahead of them. "That's where Summit House is. We've had picnics there. It used to be . . ." How could she say it used to be an old hotel, where the famous opera singer Jenny Lind had stayed? What did it matter what it was then? The question was—*What is it now?*

Callie knew there was a trail that went from the parking

lot, passing along several rock cliffs that overlooked the Connecticut River and the whole Valley. It opened into a terrace called Titan's Piazza. Nicky used to call it Titan's Pizza, which always made Mars laugh. She gulped, thinking of them both, her little brother, her older brother. How often she'd complained about being the middle child. The midden child, she'd called it, when she discovered that *midden* meant "a garbage dump." She'd give anything to be in the middle, the meat in the family sandwich, to have both of them here and safe right now. Sudden tears sprang into her eyes. Knuckling them away with one hand, she followed after Scott.

"Do you think . . . ?" she began, and couldn't finish the sentence.

"Don't think," he whispered. "And don't talk."

She shut her lips together tight and stumbled after him.

Now she could hear the flute again, full and clear, and below it, a kind of muffled sound. It took her a moment to realize it was the sound of children whimpering.

She didn't take in that they were unhappy, cold, tired, scared. What Callie heard was that they were alive.

Alive!

Letting go of Scott's hand, she plunged ahead, up onto the cliff's edge where the Summit House stood, white in the moonlight.

GRINGRAS SAT ON THE PORCH railing playing his flute. When he saw Callie, he took the flute from his lips, and smiled. It was a smile that seemed compounded of sadness and delight.

"The little reporter," he cried out as if genuinely happy to see her. "Who saw the rats dance to my piping. Look, Alabas, we have an extra. Do you think my father will give me credit against my next teind?"

Standing with his back to a door, Alabas didn't bother to answer. He looked bored, or tired, or both.

Callie took a deep breath, rehearsing what she needed to say before actually saying it. "Peter Piper," she cried at last, "I've come to take the children home."

If she had expected shock, horror, annoyance, magic, she got none of them. Gringras simply threw his head back and laughed. It was not a wicked laugh, which made it all the harder to bear.

"I *mean* it," Callie shouted.

Gringras stopped laughing. "I'm sure you do, my little reporter, but I have no choice. Really. Gold or silver or souls, you see. And the manager of the concert stole all my gold and silver, so I am—as you say in this century—stuck. But no one will be hurt. I promise."

Callie stared into the gloom behind him and could see nothing but darkness. Yet she could hear voices, sad little voices. Sad little lost voices.

"Nicky!" she cried.

The only answer she got was a wave of sound, like weeping, but no one came forward out of the darkness.

"Nicky," she cried again.

Then Alabas leaped over the side of the porch, his face the color of old porcelain in the moonlight. Shaking his head, he came over and put his hand on her arm. "You'll like it in Faerie," he said. "It's always the weekend, never school.

There's laughter and music, dancing and wine and . . ."

"I'm not old enough for wine," Callie said, trying to look over his shoulder to the weeping blackness behind Gringras. All the while she thought, *Faerie? We're going to Faerie?* She tried to remember what Granny Kirkpatrick said about them. "The People of Peace," she called them. "Though they are hardly that."

Just then Scott stepped into the clearing.

"Ah." Gringras shifted around so that both his feet dangled over the side of the railing. He held the flute loosely in his right hand. "Scott, come to find the truth after all these years?"

"What have you done with the children?" Scott asked.

"What have you done with your adolescence?" Gringras shot back.

Scott was strangely silent at that and Callie couldn't think why.

"Perhaps," Gringras said, his legs swinging back and forth, "now is the time to tell you the whole story."

"A story?" Scott and Callie spoke as one. "Now?"

"A good reporter always wants the story, does she not?"

Gringras waved his flute at her as though it were a magic wand and she shied from it. When nothing magical happened, she nodded, and said boldly, "Even if she never gets to tell the story to anyone." *Listen carefully, Callie,* she warned herself. *All our lives may depend upon it.*

"The story of a prince of the Fey, a prince of the Sidhe, the Fair Folk, the Ever Fair, the People of Peace."

"He means faeries," Alabas said.

"I mean me." Gringras' voice was suddenly low, throbbing, full of pain.

23 · Story Time

Gringras began his story by telling her about the little hillside in Faerie, where he'd been chewing on a piece of grass, thinking about billy goats gruff, middle children, and murder.

"I'm a middle kid, too!" Callie piped up. "I know how you feel." *Maybe we can connect,* she thought, though looking at his stony face she didn't believe it for a minute.

Well, maybe if I can stretch things out . . . it will give the police time to come. But in her heart she guessed they wouldn't find much. Faerie glamour would conceal everything.

Gringras stopped his narrative and stared at her straight on, as if really seeing her for the first time. "I doubt you have any idea how I feel, reporter," he said.

"My name is Callie," she told him.

He ignored her and began his tale.

Callie gasped at the part of the story when the guardian of the century plant entered the clearing. She turned and looked at Alabas in a new light after hearing of his bravery.

Alabas shrugged and leaned against the white building.

She cried out in horror at the part of the story where Gringras charged up to the pyre, and breathed a sigh of relief when Tormalas awoke unscathed. She interrupted the narrative whenever she could, punctuating it with sighs and grimaces, with coughs and giggles. But nothing really stopped the flow of his telling.

Then Gringras told of the blow that killed his brother and the story was over.

"You *killed* your own brother?" Callie asked, suddenly thinking of Nicky and thinking of Mars. Even when she felt most in the midden, she couldn't have done any such thing. Gringras was right about one thing: She had no idea at all how he was feeling.

Gringras stared down at the dark valley far below. Lost in thought, he gave only one short nod.

"What did your father say?" Callie whispered.

"Say?" Gringras barked a laugh. "Only this:

" 'Hame again ye'll ne'er be
   Till a mortal kens what faeries see,
   Till a charmed soul stays of its own free will
   And a mortal knows ye and loves ye still.
   But each se'en years by sweat of brow
   Bring silver, gold, or souls enow
   To pay the teind for a brother's death,
   Or as mortal man draw yer final breath.' "

Callie recognized the language as the same Alabas had used with the promoter. *Was that just last night?* "What does that mean in English?"

Gringras pushed himself off the porch and landed lightly next to where Callie stood. "It means I am cursed."

Cursed. Callie tried desperately to remember any stories Granny Kirkpatrick had told about curses and all she could come up with was that there was always some way out of them. The hero always found a back door. A different interpretation. Another way of thinking. A . . .

But Gringras interrupted her thoughts by grabbing her by the upper arm. Not painfully, but firmly, so that she couldn't escape. "Story time is over, mortal maiden. It is time to go. Alabas, gather the others."

He waved his free hand in a quick intricate pattern and a crowd of children emerged from the dark, like a picture slowly coming into focus. Their costumes were disheveled, dirty, torn, and they looked scared and tired. *But,* Callie reminded herself, *they're alive!*

She scanned them intently looking for Nicky. She saw Josee, silent for once, with Alison Velcroed to her side. The Napier kids were holding hands. Little Jodie Ryan sat in her wheelchair, head down. Even the Piatt kids were quiet, sullen, sorry-looking.

There! Nicky's wizard hat was gone and his robe was as dirty and torn as the others, but he was okay. Callie had never been gladder to see anyone in her life.

"Nicky!" she called to him as he stared down at his feet, dejected. "Nicky, I'm right here. Callie's here. Everything's going to be all right, Bugbrain." He didn't seem to hear her though he was only a few yards away.

Gringras nodded to Alabas and began pulling Callie around the Summit House toward the cliff face.

"Wait!" she screamed and tried to wriggle free but Gringras held her fast. She struggled and aimed a kick at him. He ignored her.

She kicked again.

And again.

If her blows were doing any damage to his long, thin legs he didn't seem to notice. She aimed her fingernails at his eyes but he shifted his head to one side and caught her free hand with his. Closing both her wrists in one of his hands, he dragged her further toward the cliff.

Suddenly, a bright light flared up and a loud rumble sounded. Scott emerged from the darkness astride his huge motorcycle.

"Scott!" Callie cried out happily. *He must have sneaked out while Gringras was telling the story,* she thought. *I'm glad one of us was thinking!*

Even in her terror, Callie noted how wonderful he looked. His Viking face was set with fierce determination and he must not have had time to put his helmet on for his long blonde hair flew back like angel wings as he bore down upon them. The bike's headlight centered on Gringras' chest, as if targeting him for a blow.

Callie was just getting ready to spring aside at the last moment, like the heroines in the movies always do, when Alabas leaped, catlike, from his spot near the wall. He caught Scott high on the shoulder, knocking him flying. The bike's motor died and it skittered, riderless, to a halt, not three feet from Callie.

After a brief scuffle, Scott and Alabas arose, a small knife in Alabas' hand an inch from Scott's eye.

"I canna let you go, Scottie," Alabas said. "Not now. Not ever. But never mind. Faerie is a great place for a musician."

Callie cried and slumped over, Gringras' hold on her wrists now the only thing keeping her standing.

Without comment, Gringras turned and continued toward the cliff, dragging Callie along while behind them marched Alabas and Scott and the long line of gray-faced children in bedraggled Halloween costumes.

"Where are we going?" Callie asked. But she knew without being told.

They were going into Faerie.

They walked up to the cliff, a solid gray rock with bands of some lighter color meandering through it like a petrified river.

Then they walked *into* the rock.

That was impossible, yet it happened. One minute they were outside the rock face, the next inside, as if they'd gone into a cave. But it was no cave. Rather, it was another world with a path and trees, and light.

At first the light seemed crepuscular, like the light that shines in the sky between sunset and night. The trees were all leafless, with bony fingers pointing up at the ever-gray sky, but there were no piles of leaves around the roots. The path was stony, well-worn, and Gringras and Alabas were careful to keep on it. So Callie was careful, too.

They walked along for an hour, maybe a bit less. The sky never seemed to get any darker nor the light any less gray. None of the trees wore leaves.

If this is Faerie, Callie thought miserably, *this gray, uneasy place, they can keep it!* But she didn't let her misery get in the way of thinking about the old stories Granny Kirkpatrick had told. About Faerie, where the People of Peace—the Ever Fair! *That was another name.* Where they lived forever. Well, at least for a long time. And, she suddenly recalled, in her grandmother's stories, the People of Peace weren't the nice guys at all. Not little, pretty winged creatures out of Disney. They were . . .

Suddenly, from far away she heard some sort of rushing sound. *Water over stone,* she thought. Then she smelled something odd, a kind of metallic odor.

"What's that?" she whispered.

No one answered, though at the sound of her voice, the line of children began to whimper.

Gringras turned around, waved his hand—the one with the ring on it—and the children went silent again.

On they walked, the stone path flintier now. Harder to walk upon. Great stone banks on either side made the pathway narrower still, forcing them into a single file, so Gringras had to let Callie's arm go.

Callie touched the wall of stone for support. It was cold, unyielding. *Like Gringras,* she thought.

Then, up ahead, the path suddenly forked into three roads. The one to the right was narrow and seemed set about with briars and thorns. The very look of it made Callie shudder. The middle road was broad and even, it looked easy to walk on. Callie thought of the poor children behind her, way past their bedtimes, scared and exhausted. She hoped Gringras would let them take that road.

The road off to the left seemed to double back on itself

again and again. Switchbacks, they were called in the real world. Callie had no idea what they'd be called in Faerie.

Checking the sky again, Callie saw it was still that gray not-quite-night color, with no sun and no moon and no stars. She dared a look behind her at the children.

Hold on, kids, she mouthed at them. She didn't dare say it aloud.

With Alabas now in the lead, his knife still at Scott's throat, they turned onto the left path, the winding one.

Remember this, Callie told herself. In case she had a chance to escape.

After three S-curves, the path suddenly opened onto the bank of a river that ran dark gray in the gray light. The metallic smell was stronger than ever, but as they approached the serpentine water, Callie saw the river wasn't gray at all. It was red.

Red as blood.

She gasped and Gringras was at her side. He grabbed her wrist and drew her right down into the flood with him. She twisted, tried to get away, but his hand was like a steel handcuff. Expecting the water to be icy cold, she was surprised when they waded knee deep through it to find it warm and sticky. Only then did she understand the metallic smell of the place. The river wasn't just red as blood—it *was* blood!

Alabas laughed and sang out, "All the blude that's shed on earth runs through the springs o' that countrie." Then he dragged Scott through the river after him and the children followed, even little Jodie Ryan in her wheelchair, being pushed by Josee.

The thought of all that blood made Callie shudder again, though when they got to the other side, she noticed that none of them was either wet or stained by the red water.

Odd, she thought. *Though no odder than anything else this night.*

"Welcome to Faerie," Gringras said. Unaccountably, he was suddenly dressed all in green with a mantle of green lined with ermine, and a jeweled cap on his head. His eyes seemed deeper, more intense, gayer. *Even,* Callie thought, *happy.* There were smile lines at the corners.

All around them birds burst into song. The sun, a shining disc of yellow, like a child's watercolor painting, rose ahead of them. Soft morning light shone across the grassy path, dappling it with gold. Apple trees to their left were in blossom, while on the right the same trees were fully ripe.

"This makes no sense," Callie said aloud.

"It is Faerie," Gringras told her, before moving away. Then he said over his shoulder, "Earth rules do not apply here."

From somewhere straight ahead came the sounds of music and laughter.

24 · Into Faerie

Now Gringras stood on the bank of the river and gazed off to where the sounds were coming from. When he looked back at Callie, his eyes were no longer happy and his voice shook when he spoke.

"I envy you, my little reporter."

"Me?" Callie asked incredulously.

"Yes, you. You get to continue on into Faerie. You will see wonders such as you have never imagined. You will live forever in the land of the Ever Fair, in the Seelie Court, a place of magicks and glamour. But this," he drew an imaginary line in front of him with his foot, which Callie noticed was now shod in green leather, "this is far as I can go."

Alabas finally sheathed his knife and came to stand next to Gringras, staring in the same direction, a similar look of longing on his face.

"Because of the curse?" Callie asked.

Gringas nodded. "We wait on the pleasure of my father now. Relax, it may be some time. He takes his pleasures slow." And to emphasize this, he sat down on the soft grass, still staring over the horizon, as if forcing his eyes to travel where his feet could not. The sun was now high overhead.

Callie had no wish to relax. She had to think. Think about her grandmother's stories, think about the curse, think about getting them all out of there. But somehow she couldn't think what to do. Trying to get Nicky's attention was as futile as before; none of the children seemed able to see her. They had been unnaturally quiet since Gringras had cast his last spell over them. She thought briefly about making a run for it but she couldn't leave Nicky behind. Or the others.

She gave a quiet, bitter little laugh. *If I couldn't escape from Gringras in the real world, what makes me think being in Faerie will make escape any easier?*

She tried to catch Scott's eye in case he had any ideas, but he was staring at his feet, much like the children. Either he had been enchanted or else he was too depressed by his easy defeat at Alabas' hands. Callie didn't know which, but it was clear he'd be no help any more.

So—we're hostages, she thought.

Putting it that way gave her some perspective. Made the unreal somehow more real. But she knew she would have to understand her situation if she hoped to get them out of it, and clearly she couldn't outfight them or outrun them. So, she'd have to outthink them.

She put her head in her hands, closed her eyes, and began to piece things together one little bit at a time, as if she were writing the story.

Why kidnap children?

To pay the teind.
Why pay the teind?
Because of the curse.

Callie looked over at Gringras who was still staring into the distance. Something came to her in a blinding flash: *Break the curse and he has no reason to take the children.*

But that brought up a bigger question. She closed her eyes again. Why hadn't he broken the curse in however many centuries he'd been walking the earth? Surely he must have tried?

Only one way to find out, she thought. *Ask.*

"How long since you were thrown out of Faerie?" She was surprised at how solid her voice sounded when she felt wispy, unfocused, scared.

Gringras tore his eyes from the horizon and pinned her with his gaze. "By your count, little reporter, nearly eight centuries."

Eight centuries! Surely he was joking. But his face said he was telling the truth. So she took a deep breath. "Do you mean you never tried to break the curse—not even once?"

"There is no breaking it; it is too powerful."

"So you never tried?"

Gringras shook his head. "Do not be intentionally stupid. Of course I have tried. Repeatedly. For the first one hundred years or so. Tried to find a mortal to love me knowing who I was, what I had done. My attempts were laughable at best, occasionally tragic. But then . . ." He shrugged and fell silent.

"Then . . . ?" Callie prompted.

"Then I just concentrated on doing what I had to do."

His mouth was a thin line, and his eyes distant. He suddenly looked as old as he claimed, like some mummy in a museum. Turning from her, he seemed to be listening to that faraway music.

"That's just another way of saying you gave up," Callie accused. "Stopped trying. Took the easy way out."

"Easy way—hah!" Gringras turned back. "I know you think me a bad man. And it is true I have done some wicked things in my time. But I do try to avoid true evil. Still, the more time I spent trying to devise ways to break the curse and its impossible conditions, the less time I spent making money. So the last centuries I concentrated on silver and gold—and succeeded. Because I knew what you now know—what happens when I fall short on silver or gold. What I am then forced to do." He pointed to the children without looking at them. "You cannot believe I enjoy this."

Callie followed his finger and stared at the children. Next to Nicky stood his best friend, Jason Piatt. And the triplets from down the block. Little Jodie Ryan in her wheelchair was crowded next to the Napiers. And what looked like an entire second grade. Further behind them she saw some older kids, like Josee and Alison, only a few in actual costumes. They must have been taking the little ones around to all the houses.

Suddenly Callie was filled with despair: for them, for herself, for the whole situation. She choked back a sob. "If you don't enjoy it, then why can't you just let us go?" she pleaded.

Gringras responded in a monotone. "Next question."

Sniffling, Callie tried to gather herself. Gave up trying. It was too hard. It was impossible . . . and then she realized. *I am doing just what Gringras did. Giving up. And no hero in Granny Kirkpatrick's stories ever acted that way.* She gave herself a shake. *Break the curse!* That's what had to be done. If she couldn't remember how it was done in the stories, she would find a way here, in real life.

Sitting up, Callie said carefully, "So, besides a mortal loving you, what are these 'impossible conditions'?"

Gringras smiled slowly and without warmth, then began to chant:

"Hame again ye'll ne'er be
 Till a mortal kens what faeries see,
 Till a charmed soul stays of its own free will
 And a mortal knows ye and loves ye still."

He was about to explain it further, when Alabas spoke up. "Your father approaches."

Gringras nodded and stood.

Reluctantly, Callie followed suit. If Gringras couldn't think of an answer, perhaps his father could. She was surprised that the faeries were so close. She'd been concentrating so hard on questioning Gringras that she hadn't noticed that the music and laughter had gotten nearer. Now she could hear thundering drums and bleating horns as a strange procession crested a small hill.

Callie stared, agog, at the faerie court. Some of them walked, some flew, and others rode creatures as bizarre as themselves. The leading courtiers carried multi-colored banners on which things were written in an old-fashioned script. Several of them had musical instruments. Besides the drums and horns, there were long wooden flutes, an odd hand harp, and a kind of small bagpipes. One stork-legged man juggled balls of fire and two of the winged fairies had crystal balls floating before them.

And then there were the children—human children. Dozens of them, like little forlorn ghosts, white-faced, the sun shining right through them. They were dressed in rags of old-fashioned costumes, some clearly peasants wearing clogs. Several seemed highborn, in tattered velvet jackets and high leather boots that were scuffed and worn. Two little boys in silken nightshirts and nightcaps held hands and danced along barefooted.

The entire troop gamboled and sang, their approach a directionless, chaotic ramble that still brought them closer and closer to where Callie and the others waited.

In the center of this mad throng, astride a huge black horse, rode an older version of Gringras. The same thin face, the same piercing eyes, the same high cheekbones and mirthless smile. He wore robes of royal purple and a white ermine cloak. Atop his head perched a silver jeweled crown. By his side, on a gray mare, was a woman whose hair was bound up in ribbons and jewels.

That must be King Merrias, Callie thought. And the queen.

When they got within ten yards, the king raised his hand and the parade halted as one. The music died, juggling balls disappeared, and flag-posts were planted into the ground. Even the wind seemed to obey and the banners fell slack as the wind died.

"Aren't they beautiful?" breathed Scott, lifting his eyes from the ground for the first time in an hour.

Callie took a closer look. There were small, warty creatures with red hats, and lithe humanoids who almost disappeared when they turned sideways. There were tall, slim folk with white hair and violet eyes, as well as hummingbird-sized fairies with translucent wings. Small, naked brownies stood side by side to giraffe-high trolls with slack jaws and too many teeth. Living balls of light illuminated the craggy faces of deformed dwarfish brutes. Normal-looking men and women suddenly turned into dogs and back again at the blink of an eye, and one even flopped around as a seal for a moment before thinking better of it and popping back into human form.

In a movie, Callie thought, *they might be fascinating. Great action figures for a Happy Meal. But here, up close, and way too personal, they're something out of a nightmare.*

Even the king, who, at first glance, was as good-looking as his son, seemed cold and distant and much too inhuman to be considered beautiful.

"No," Callie said, turning to Scott, "they aren't beautiful at all. They're mean and old and ugly. And they want to keep us here forever." *Forever,* she thought. *And if I don't figure out this curse now, I might—like Gringras—just give up.*

Scott didn't seem to hear her. He kept staring, rapt.

However, Gringras *did* hear, and he spun Callie around by her shoulders to face him. He said, with a strange wild hope, "What did you say?"

Callie, confused, answered, "They aren't beautiful."

"What *do* you see?" Gringras asked.

So, as King Merrias and his queen looked imperiously down at them, Callie described the court as best she could—the small warty folk and the large troll men, the winged fairies and the rest.

"You see them as I do!" Gringras said excitedly when she'd finished. He let out a long breath. "Reporter Callie," he continued, his eyes alarmingly wide, "if it meant that your brother could go free, would you stay here in Faerie voluntarily?"

Callie glanced over at Nicky. He still looked so lost and frightened, his wizard robe covered with dirt and fall leaves. She remembered suddenly the time when he'd been barely a year old and had come down with a fever. Though just eight herself, she hadn't let her mother take her from his room. She'd slept on the floor next to his crib all that night and the next until he was better. Just as Mars had done the time she'd gotten the chicken pox. Then she remembered how Nicky had looked in his Batman jammies on the morning before he was taken. She regretted all the mean or petty things she'd said to him over the past few days. She couldn't remember now why she had been so angry with him—he was her only little brother and she loved him. Had loved him from the moment he'd been born.

"Yes," she answered at last. "Yes, I would stay."

Gringras was visibly shaking now and his grip on her shoulders was almost painful. "C-C-Cal . . . lie," he stuttered, "do you love me?"

"What?" Callie replied, shocked. She shook his hands off with an angry shudder, then loudly, definitely, even defiantly she added, "Of course not!"

Gringras' face fell and his pale complexion reddened.

Callie began ticking things off on her fingers. "One . . . you kidnapped me, my brother, and all our neighbors and friends. Two . . . you're responsible for the abduction of who knows how many children over the years. Three . . . you killed your own brother."

His face completely red now and his lips white as he pressed them together, Gringras turned his back on her.

"Four—you aren't even human. And," Callie said and she poked him in the back with her four outstretched fingers, "you're nearly eight hundred years old. I'm fourteen. That's *sick*."

Gringras seemed ready to expire from acute embarrassment. He shook his head and waved his left hand at her, trying to stop the onslaught.

About to come up with some more pointed things to say about his character, Callie stopped when she heard laughter.

It was Alabas. He was laughing, laughing from the belly, loud and raucously. Each time he seemed about to catch his breath, he would look up and see Gringras standing, red-faced, and he would burst into another fit.

"What's got into him?" Callie asked.

Gringras didn't reply but, giving a cold glare to Alabas, he stomped off down the riverbank.

On his horse, King Merrias watched this whole display without any visible emotions. Not a sparkle of amusement or anger dented his stone-like visage. Taking their cue from him, his entourage shuffled about a little but said nothing. Only the queen looked different, a spasm of something like grief passing over her beautiful face.

Alabas finally got his laughter under control and wandered up to Callie.

"Little reporter," he told her, "all my many years I have never heard anyone talk to Gringras in that way. Even his mother did not scold him like that when he was a boy." He chuckled again and seemed in danger of resuming his laughing fit. "Though it might have done him good."

"But why would he ask me those things?"

"It is the curse," said Alabas, and he chanted four lines from the now-familiar verse:

"Hame again ye'll ne'er be
 Till a mortal kens what faeries see,
 Till a charmed soul stays of its own free will
 And a mortal knows ye and loves ye still."

"I can make sense of most of it," Callie said, "but what is *hame*? And *kens*?"

"*Hame* is home. 'Home again you'll never be.' And *kens* means knows or understands. Apparently you can see through the glamour the Seelie Court have cast about themselves. You see them as we do. You 'ken what faeries see,' though I wonder how you do it."

She thought a minute. "Maybe . . ." she said slowly, "maybe it was the music." Then she added, "Scott's guitar."

Alabas nodded. "Of course."

Thinking so hard her forehead furrowed, Callie suddenly said, "So, the charmed soul is me?" She nodded to herself with understanding. "He thinks if I volunteer to stay that would count as staying of my own free will? But there's nothing free about it. It's a will forced upon me. I doubt that would save him."

Alabas nodded back. "As for the third clause, Gringras told you his life story. You know him now—as a mortal. If you could only love him, he believes it would break the curse. This is as close as we have come since we were exiled to finding a way out of this impasse. But, judging by the look on your face when he asked, it is as close as we will get today." And Alabas broke into a fresh bout of laughing.

Callie didn't feel like laughing. She was tired and scared and now she was beginning to get angry as well. Was there nothing she could do? She didn't know much about love— had never even had a crush till Scott had come along—but she was pretty sure she couldn't *make* herself love someone. And certainly not the fairy prince, for all his unearthly beauty.

What she wanted to do was to sit back down on the bank of the river of blood and cry or yell or scream. She wanted to wake up at her desk and have this all be a bad dream. Most of all she wanted to give up. To throw her hands in the air and say, "Okay! You win!" But she couldn't. The kids might not know it, but she was their best hope. The only way she could think of to save them, though, was to ask more questions. The more she knew about the situation, the better chance she had—if there *was* a better chance! She bit her lip and tried to think of what else she needed to know.

At last she asked, "Why does the king sit there, not speaking?" and waited for Alabas to get his laughter under control.

"We have to send our teind to him by nightfall. It has become a game to Gringras. He waits till the last minute to see if he can get the king to speak to him." Alabas shrugged. "They are a stubborn family. Eight hundred earth years and the old man has never said a word to Gringras, though the queen blanches at the silence and tears drop from her eyes like rain."

"And what happens if you don't pay up by nightfall?"

"*'As a mortal man draw yer final breath,'*" Alabas answered with a line from the curse. "We become like you. Mortal."

Callie had run out of questions.

And the sun, once high in the sky, was finally growing lower.

She knew she was running out of time as well.

25 · Curses

Callie drew in a deep breath and walked away from Gringras and Alabas. She wanted to think about curses, and being next to the two of them seemed to keep her from thinking clearly, as if her mind were becoming increasingly foggy.

She found a rock, gray, solid, shaped like a sofa, and sat down.

In her world curses were swears, words that got you sent to your room. But here, in Faerie, curses were the real thing. something that could condemn you to a kind of living death, or a death in life. She shuddered.

Then she remembered Granny Kirkpatrick's stories again. About how there was always another way out. She thought it must be true. It *had* to be true—or there was no hope.

And a mortal knows ye and loves ye still.

Surely she wasn't the only mortal who had ever known Gringras. There were all those band members over the centuries. But had they been part of the glamour or apart from it?

She looked around. Scott and Nick and all the kids from the neighborhood were as bespelled as before. It must have always been like that. No mortal ever really had a chance to know the faerie prince. They would have been glamoured, mesmerized, hypnotized, glazed. Men, women, children—Gringras had used them but had never let them get close. Close was dangerous. But, Callie knew this with sudden and utter certainty, close was also the only way to be saved.

As if they knew what she was thinking, the little ghostly children of the Seelie Court suddenly surrounded her rock, speaking to her in wispy voices, more like the sound of wind through leaves than any real conversation. They plucked at her hair and clothes, as if assuring themselves that she was human and not fey.

She let them pick at her, because she hardly felt a thing. Their touch was like little summer breezes brushing her face, her hair, her jeans, not like human fingers at all.

The children spoke as if out of storybooks, the kinds of stories with kings and knights and lonely princesses casked up in towers awaiting rescue. She heard, "My liege," and "la-dykins," "God's wounds" and "S'blood," and "canst thou, canst thou not" and "zounds!" The words were odd, old-fashioned, foreign-sounding. She heard "kith and kin," "converse," "fortnight," and "teind."

"Teind!" she said aloud. That one, at least, made sense to her.

The ghost children buzzed and plucked about her even more till the tallest of the nightshirt boys, standing behind the rest, raised his hand.

"Silence!" he said clearly and with authority, though still in a whispery voice. He was a handsome boy, about her age, his fair hair a lighter gray and pushed back from his eyes.

The ghost children stood still, quiet, waiting.

Coming forward, the boy stared down at Callie. "Canst see us true?"

She nodded. "If you're a boy in a nightshirt and bare feet I can."

He drew himself up and said in his wind-voice, "I am a *prince* in a nightshirt and bare feet."

She nodded. "I can see that now, your majesty."

"And wilt thou make obeisance to me?"

This, she thought, *is the oddest conversation I've ever had.* But the whole night had been odd. So she said matter-of-factly, "If you mean will I bow to you, the answer is no, because I'm an American. We don't have royalty here."

"Here," he said, just as matter-of-factly, "be Faerie."

"Ah. . . ." She bowed at the waist.

"Hast come, lady, to break the spell and take us home?" It was the smaller nightshirted boy, coming forward, and slipping his hand in his brother's.

Callie wondered if she was to bow to him, too. But before she could attempt any such thing, all the ghost children gathered around again, touching her—though this time their touches seemed different somehow: pleading, begging, desperate.

"I have told thee and told thee," the prince said, turning to them, "that though we mayhap be freed someday, none of us will be vouchsafed a journey home."

"Why not?" Callie asked aloud.

"What the year, lady?" the boy asked in return.

"Two thousand and . . ." Callie began but the gray children did not let her finish. Some of them screamed, little tatters of sound, others put their hands to their ears. Still others turned to their neighbors, asking frantic questions in their strange, foreign languages.

Finally the prince said, "I am Edward, lady, prince of Wales. I was to have been king after my father, who died in the year of Our Lord 1483. Murdered, so I wot. But I was stolen from my bed in the Tower along with my younger brother, Dickie here."

Callie nodded.

"It was the piper and his man, hired by that rogue Richard to play at his usurped coronation."

Callie leaned forward. "Hired to kill you?"

The little prince nodded. "But he did not, lady. The faerie prince does not hold with murder."

"Except of his own brother," Callie said.

The young prince nodded. "So thou seest true."

She saw even more than that. "1483? You would be long . . ." She couldn't say more, trying desperately to disguise the horror and sadness she suddenly felt.

The older prince nodded. "I have tried to explain to these peasants, but none of them is bright enough to truly understand—once we set foot back on the soil of earth, we will no longer be bespelled by Faerie. We will become our proper ages."

"But you'd be . . ." Callie gasped, trying to figure out how old he was. She knew it had to be hundreds.

He said it for her. "We'd be hundreds of years old and turned to dust, free only to become motes of sunlight, shards of memory, floating to Heaven," the little prince said, "for none of us be old enough or evil enough to be flung down to perdition."

"But not go home?" Dickie asked, his lower lip trembling. "Not to see mother again?" Tears shimmered in his eyes.

"Then I stay!" a girl cried out from the crowd of gray children, shaking her head which set her little braids swinging. "Better here alive in death than a dust mote on earth."

"And I!" another called, a boy, raising his hand.

"And I. . . ." An agreement rang all around the grey mob.

The prince of Wales turned to them, and this time his voice was almost full strength. "And let Faerie win? Never! We must leave, and God will speed us on our way to Heaven."

"Wait," Callie said, "I don't understand. If I stay to love Gringras, to sacrifice myself, will I have actually saved anyone? I mean, my brother, my neighbors . . ." She pointed over to them. "Or will they be dust motes, too?"

"The river of time runs differently here," the young prince said. "But this place on which we now stand is not yet Faerie proper where time stops altogether. Once thee leaves *this* place, lady, this borderlands, mayhap a day has become a year, an afternoon a lifetime. But I cannot say for certain."

Which means, Callie thought, *I have to figure out things now. Before midnight. Before we are taken into Faerie proper.*

At that moment, Alabas came over and the gray children scattered before him, like little mice before the cat. "So you have met them, the teinds. What do you think of them?" His eyes were hooded now and she felt he was toying with her.

"Is it true that if they leave, they will be dust motes?" she asked.

"What is true is that they are hundreds of years old." He had the grace not to smile. "But here in Faerie they stay young forever. Is that not a boon?"

Callie thought a minute. "But *you* have grown up, Alabas. *You* haven't stayed young forever. Gringras' brother died. Someone will succeed the king."

Now Alabas smiled, his teeth small and even and very white. "You are quick, little reporter. Yes, we of the Seelie Court age in Faerie, but at a rate much slower than folk in the outside world. Accidents can happen here. And murder. Even war. But those on whom we put a glamour, do not change at all as long as they remain. They cannot change. The magic will not let them. The energy of their human youth is what keeps Faerie going. It is a kind of power. It works as electricity does in your world."

"And you want me here as well."

Callie wasn't asking a question, but he answered anyway, shaking his finger at her. "We *have* you here as well."

"*You* don't," she told him. "The king does. *You* are doomed to live in my world."

He laughed. "It has its advantages."

"Name one."

"It has Gringras."

And then she knew. The back door. The escape. The answer. Granny Kirkpatrick had been right. There was one.

It had been there all along. Only it was so simple, Gringras and Alabas had never thought of it. Or they had been too selfish, too sure of themselves, too focused on being saved by some mortal, who they would despise because—after all—they were of Faerie. But the solution was so far-fetched and so . . . she chuckled to herself . . . near-fetched, they'd never even considered it.

Callie leaned forward and said softly, "You love him. You love Gringras."

"He is my prince," Alabas said carefully. "My liege."

"He's your best friend."

"My *only* friend."

For the first time since this awful evening had begun, Callie smiled.

26 · Revenge

Gringras crouched on his heels and fumed, vainly trying to get his temper under control. The human girl humiliating him in front of his father was bad enough, but it was Alabas' laughter that had really stung him. He hadn't heard his friend laugh freely like that in—literally—centuries and he certainly hadn't expected to be the target of it when it finally came.

When had Alabas turned so serious? *Gringras thought.* For that matter, when did I?

He recalled them laughing all the time in the days of their youth. Childhood is long in the land of the Ever Fair, and they had taken full advantage of it, torturing their nannies and tutors with pranks. Even their plan to overthrow Tormalas— before its tragic end—had seemed the grandest prank of all. And a tweak on the nose for Gringras' dour father.

Gringras glanced at the king sitting stone-faced and motionless on his horse. Suddenly he had an odd thought: Father was once a child like me. *It was an uncomfortable thought.* Before he became the gargoyle he is now, Father must have run and laughed and played like any child.

As often happens when such a thought presented itself, Gringras immediately put it to song. He chanted aloud:

> *"Unmoving, unchanging, a statue alone,*
> *No wind nor weather, can alter the stone."*

As he nodded in cadence to the brand-new lines, the thrill he still got from putting together a rhyme almost broke him out of his bleak mood. But another thought struck him. And now, I have become him.

Staring at his father, Gringras had the urge to pluck a piece of grass and chew it on it as he used to do when he was much younger. If only because it was something he couldn't picture his father ever doing.

No, *he thought, reconsidering,* I have not become him. I have become worse. *His throat felt tight, as if at any moment he might weep.*

> *"For stone cannot weep, and stone cannot feel,*
> *Emotions are left to the mortal and real."*

He smiled bitterly at the irony. For now he was almost mortal himself, and almost overwhelmed with feelings. Most of what he felt, though, was fury. At his father and at himself.

My father, *he thought,* may be a humorless, vicious, stone statue of a king, but everything he does, he does for one reason: the kingdom. Me? Everything I do is for myself. *His thoughts came tumbling out in a frenzy.*

I am selfish and weak. *He very nearly began ticking off his faults on his fingers like Callie had done but caught himself and clenched his fists instead.* My fear of my father and my fear of becoming mortal have turned me into a coward. *His mouth twisted with self-loathing.* I am more than a coward. I am evil. I can try to blame my actions on the curse, but the fact remains: I do evil things. Therefore I must be evil.

Standing, his thousand year old limbs creaking for the first time in his life, he suddenly felt tired and old. He unclenched his fists and marched unsteadily toward his father and his magical retinue. Getting as close as he could, Gringras leaned into the enchantment as if it were a strong wind keeping him from falling forward.

The king met his gaze unblinkingly.

If I am evil, *he thought again,* so be it. But I will no longer be a coward. *Silently, he held his fist up to his father.* If I cannot break the curse with mortal love then I will break it with mortal force. I am done lurking in shadows and stealing children. I am done playing for my supper.

He tried to get his father to look away but knew it was futile. The old man was a stone. Gringras realized he was shaking.

"Old man," he cried out, "I have the teind you demand which gives me seven more years. But when next I return, it will be with a mortal army at my back. I will fight my way in or die in the attempt. But I *will come home.*"

The king said nothing; his face said nothing. He had held his hand up pinkie and point fingers extended.

The queen wept silently.

Gringras spun away and stared into the distance over the

heads of Alabas and the teinds. He envisioned himself astride a
black horse like his father's, at the head of a million charmed
souls, all carrying weapons the denizens of Faerie had never
seen before.

In his vision, he shouts a single order and guns fire, filling the
air with cold steel. Jets and bombers, manned by blank-eyed hu-
man pilots, scream overhead, spewing flame. Tanks roll onto the
ever-golden fields of Faerie crushing meadow wort, tansy, mus-
tard seed, and fern. Machine guns and mortars spray screaming
fairies till their wings catch fire and burn. Gringras dismounts
his black horse and wades into the gore, his sword flashing in the
dying sun.

"I will come home," he repeated under his breath, eyes still
afire with what he had seen in his vision. "Even if I have to
empty every city on earth and burn Faerie to the ground to do it."

More time had passed than Gringras had realized, for the
setting sun had almost reached the horizon. Time to send the
teind across for this seven years. But now that he knew what lay
ahead, seven years seemed hardly any time at all.

"Gringras!" Alabas called to him. He sounded strange,
hopeful.

Gringras shook his head to lose the farsight that was upon
him and saw Alabas and the girl, Callie, running toward him.

Now why do they look so excited? *he wondered.* Why do
they look hopeful when surely they know that now, with
what I have planned, all hope is gone.

27 · The Buying of Freedom

The prince of the Sidhe turned toward them with a face that looked as if it had been set in concrete. Callie couldn't wait to see it turn flesh again when they told him how he could buy his way back into Faerie. How the curse could be broken.

For the first time since she found out that Nicky was missing, she felt she could breathe, as though some iron band around her chest had been cut.

"Gringras," Alabas called, his voice as light as if it had wings.

Gringras all but snarled at them. "The old stone man waits his teind. It is time."

"In fact, it is all the time in the world," Alabas said, opening his arms and trying to embrace the prince.

Gringras shook him off. "What cant is this? What game?"

"No game," Callie assured him. "I . . . I have figured the way out of the curse."

Gringras laughed bitterly. "I have figured it out, too. We

pay the teind and be gone from here." He paused. "And in seven years . . ."

Hands up as if in prayer, Alabas said in a pleading voice, "Please, my prince, the girl has the right of it."

"I do not believe it," Gringras said. "A mortal could not figure it out in a million years, not if a prince of Faerie has broken his heart on it."

"Just listen," Alabas said.

Without waiting for his response, Callie began.

"Hame again ye'll ne'er be
  Till a human kens what faeries see,
  Till a charmed soul stays of its own free will
  And a mortal knows ye and loves ye still."

"Her accent is execrable," said Gringras.

"Oh, for the gods' sake, shut up and listen," Alabas cried.

Shocked, Gringras shut his mouth, his lips in a thin slash. Clearly it was rare that Alabas spoke that way to him.

Callie spoke hurriedly, "If you don't deliver the goods this night, you and Alabas will have to go back into the world and live mortal lives, right?"

Grudgingly, Gringras nodded.

"You and Alabas. You will be *mortals!*" She was silent for a moment to let that sink in. "And then, as a mortal who knows you and loves you still, *Alabas* could lead you back home to Faerie."

A light, like a will-o'-the-wisp, lit Gringras' eyes. It grew larger, brighter, till his eyes seemed candled from within. He gasped, clapped his hands, laughed out loud. "Oh, little reporter, how have you figured this out in a night when I have had an eternity?" He struck himself on the chest with the flat of his hand. "But here, in the seat of all emotion—human or fey—I know that what you say is true. The mortal Alabas will lead me home. The heart knows its own. The curse seems already lighter. My elven soul takes wing." Then, suddenly, he sobered. "But what of the rest? The charmed soul staying in Faerie of its own free will?"

Callie smiled, though there was no humor in it. "I think you'll have little trouble with that one, great prince of the Fey. From what I hear, not all of the teinds want to go back to earth with the little princes from the tower. The oldest of them fear they will only become dust motes."

Gringras nodded, and Callie thought, *So it is true. All that awaits them is freedom without return.* Sadness, like nausea, threatened to overwhelm her. *The faerie folk have no consciences,* she thought. *They don't care. They aren't People of Peace. They aren't Fair Folk. They are cruel and careless and callous.* Of course she said none of this aloud, saying instead, "Promise to free them within Faerie, and you may make yourself a whole new following."

Gringras picked her up and spun her around. He kissed her on the forehead and tiny silver stars seemed to ring her head.

"Not me, *Gringras.* I won't be glamoured." She scrubbed at her forehead with the back of her right hand.

Laughing, Alabas said, "She will not, you know. The strings of Scott's guitar ring through her true."

Carefully Gringras set her on the ground and turned. "Father," he cried out to the stone man on the horse, "I shall not be giving you these teinds tonight." Then he looked over his shoulder. "Alabas, lead them back to the human world. But hurry. The old man may take what he is not offered."

King Merrias smiled grimly but did not otherwise shift his seat. His voice boomed out, emotionless, over the clearing. "My son has chosen to release the teind. He knows the consequence to himself—mortality. He and his companion will live and die as humans, whose lives are as brief to us as a Mayfly is to them." Then pulling on the reins, he brought his horse around. Without a backward glance, he left to go along the path into Faerie.

The weeping queen followed. Behind them gamboled the faerie folk: boggarts and phookas, and winged sprites and all. Callie watched until the last of them had disappeared.

"Come, child," Gringras said and held his hand out to Callie. "I will take you back to earth."

"I know the way," Callie said. "You wait here for Alabas to return. I wish I could see your father's face when you tell him."

"It will not change him," Gringras told her. "But my mother, at least, will weep no more."

"Your mother," Callie pointed out brutally, "is still one son short."

She was pleased to see that he blanched at her words.

CALLIE HAD BEEN TELLING THE truth when she said she remembered the way. She followed the serpentine river of blood that smelled both salty and metallic, until she came to the fording place.

Wading the river, she found it chilly this time. On getting out, she saw that her jeans had been stained a strange purple color, and her white Nikes were now bloodred.

The flinty path proved a difficult climb, until up ahead she saw the dust coming up from the shoes of the travelers ahead of her. She began running then, until the breath hurt in her lungs and she had an ache in her side. "Wait," she cried out. "Wait for me."

The mist cleared, and there were the children, just a whiney bunch of ordinary kids, a bit tattered and filthy and weary from a long midnight hike.

When she made out Nicky's form, she ran to him, picked him up, spun him around, and kissed him on the forehead. Then she laughed, relieved there were no little stars around his head.

"Callie!" he said, his face going all puckered, as if he were going to start crying. "Where *were* you? Where *are* we?"

"We were in dreamland, Bugbrain," she said. "And now we're almost home." Up ahead stood a great wall of stone.

Alabas pointed to it. "Go through there," he said, "and you will be on the mountain."

"And you?"

"Back to Gringras. And Faerie. And home."

She smiled. "May you get what you wish."

Alabas shook his head. "One must always be careful what one wishes for," he said. "Especially in Faerie."

"Then may you get what you deserve," she said.

"I suspect that would be even worse!" He laughed. And then he was gone.

The stone had become an arched door outlined with a

shimmering light. When they walked through it, Callie in the lead holding Nicky by the hand, the children found themselves in the parking lot near the Summit House, with the sun just rising pink and normal through the trees. For a moment they were surrounded by dust motes, little grains of light that spiraled upward toward that sky.

Callie put a hand over her heart. She knew that the motes were those little stolen children of the past who had chosen to return and who were even now heading toward Heaven.

"Godspeed," Callie whispered and raised a hand. She had no idea how many of them were now gone, but she was sure that the princes of the tower were among them.

The younger Elm Street children started sobbing then. Josee and Alison did what they could to comfort them, Josee by jabbering and making funny faces, and Alison by giving them hugs. But Callie looked around for the one face she hadn't seen since they'd come through the gate from Faerie.

"Scott?" she cried, over the chaos and babble. "Scott, where are you?"

"Here."

A man was pulling Scott's motorcycle out of the bushes. He had long graying hair, and a face that was lined with hard living.

"Who are *you?*" Callie asked, still holding on to her brother's hand.

"Callie, I'm Scott," he said.

"But . . . but . . . you're old." She could feel her mouth drop open.

"The glamour is gone, that's all. I'm no longer protected

from aging by Gringras and his magic." He shrugged. "You see me now as I really am. Not exactly old, but thirty-eight. I was seventeen when I joined the band and Gringras kept me young for twenty-one years."

"With glamour?"

"With glamour. Only I didn't understand it really."

"Thirty-eight is almost as old as our parents," Nicky blurted out.

Callie felt cold.

Looking down at his fingers, flexing them, Scott smiled. "Alright then, old. But still a good musician." Reaching into a bag on the cycle, he fished out a cell phone. "What's your number, Callie?"

She told him.

He dialed the phone, then handed it to her. Mars answered on the first ring, crying.

"What are you doing home?" she asked.

"Breaking speed records," he answered. "Only one ticket. It was worth the trip. Where are you?"

Quickly she told him where they could be found. "We're all fine, Mars. *All of us*. Tell Mom and Dad. Tell *all* the parents. No one is hurt. Just tired and—confused. I'm sorry I ran off without telling anyone where I was going. But I couldn't stop. Not till I got Nicky back."

"I love you, Carrots," he said. "I'll be there soon. In a police car."

"Make it a bus," she said. "There are a lot of us here. Oh, and I love you, too." Then she hung up.

"Kids!" she shouted, silencing them all. "I've told them where we are. We'll be rescued soon."

A cheer went up, and Josee said to her, "We're already rescued. Now we just have to be picked up and carted home."

At her words, the children all breathed, "Home . . ." before silence and exhaustion fought with elation and won.

Scott took the phone back, then got on his bike. "My presence will only complicate things here."

She nodded. It was going to be hard enough explaining how they all got to the top of Mt. Holyoke, miles away from their neighborhood, without an old musician hanging around.

"Thanks," she said. "For everything."

"No—thank *you*, Callie. You saved us all. Just a little girl, but a hero all the same."

"Hey—not so little." She gave him a small smile. "Sounds like a song."

"It's a beginning," he said. "I never wrote any for the band. That was Gringras' role. He was . . . very jealous of his ability, you know."

Cocking her head to one side, she said, "Princes are like that, I guess." Then she added, "Especially princes of Faerie."

"Listen, I'll . . . I'll let you know when I'm playing round here next." He grinned shyly at her, more like a sixteen year old than a mature man.

She bit her lower lip, doubting either one of them wanted to see the other again. Not with that age difference. "Sure."

Then she watched as he gunned the motorcycle and headed off down the road. The sound of his bike was the only thing she could hear on the mountain for a long time. But once it faded, everything went silent again.

"Who was that man?" Nicky whispered. "Will he come back for us?"

She shook her head. "I don't think so, Nicky. But it's okay. Mom and Dad will be here soon. With the police."

She thought briefly of the article she'd write for class once she'd had a good night's sleep. The opening line was already firmly in her head: *The piper caught sight of the river long before the sound of rushing water reached his ears or the salt smell of blood struck his nose.* Shaking her head, she scolded herself. No one would believe such a thing. She'd have to call it fiction. A fiction made up entirely of fact. Was there a word for that? *Faction,* maybe?

Then, sitting down with Nicky, Jason Piatt, little Jodie Ryan, Josee and Alison, the Napier kids, and the rest, she waited for someone to come and get them and take them the rest of the way home.

28 - And After

It was the evening of yet another warm spring day in Faerie and Gringras sat with his good friend Alabas on a small rise overlooking a field.

The field no longer sprouted purple and red flowers, nor did feylings hover over it breathing in the sustaining aroma bouquet. The Unseelie war had flattened the field into dried mud and the feylings had been replaced by a gaggle of gray-faced children who followed Gringras wherever he went, muttering accusations at his back.

"Well, you got your wish, your majesty," Alabas said. "Though I warned the little reporter that one must be careful about what one wishes for."

Pulling a well-chewed wheat stalk out of his mouth, Gringras replied, "I should have remembered that myself." For he had gotten his wish: Wynn had died in the war, run through by an Unseelie sword, and Gringras was now heir to the throne.

"I miss my brothers, Alabas," he said and Alabas nodded in sympathy. "And I miss earth."

"What?" Alabas cried out, shocked.

Gringras nodded. "That's right. The dirt, the noise, the pain." He looked at the gray children stomping rusty swords and armor into the mud in the field below him. "I miss it all—its energy, charge, and challenge. Even this Faerie war is but a pale shadow of earth wars. Did you know I have not written any new songs since our return?"

"S'truth?"

"Not a verse, not a chorus, not a single line. Nothing." Gringras stood and dusted himself off. "We spent too much time amongst them, Alabas. It has ruined me for Faerie."

"This feeling will pass."

"Perhaps," Gringras said and shrugged. "But if it does not—and soon—then I think we shall have to visit mortal lands again."

"I hope you are joking, my lord."

"I never joke anymore, either." Gringras stood, and turned his back on the field. Then, as the sun set on another warm spring day in Faerie, he marched back to his father's castle, his one true friend and a horde of ghostly children following close behind.

∾ Brass Rat Songs ∾

UNDER THE HILL

Under the hill, under the stone,
No one can touch me for I am alone,
No one can reach me, no one can dare,
No one can love me, and I do not care.
     I do not care, for I am a stone,
     No one can touch me, for I am alone.

Shadows behind me, shadows ahead,
Shadows inside me, the quick and the dead.
No one beside me, no one can see
I am alone with the shadow of me.
     But I do not care, for I am a stone,
     No one can touch me, for I am alone.

Do not be sorry, do not bemoan,
I do not care, for I am a stone,
I am a boulder, I am a crag,
I am a mountain, a massif, a slag.
     And I do not care, for I am a stone,
     No one can touch me, for I am alone.

OUT OF THE DARKNESS

Out of the darkness and into the light,
We search for a chance to get into the fight.

Out of the starkness of love gone awry
We mumble and stumble, set wings—and then fly.

> For no one knows our pain
> No sympathy, no gain,
> And here we come, here we come
> Out of the darkness
> Again.

Out of the blackness and into the dawn,
Blink at the light as the nighttime is gone.
Out of the blankness of awe-filled despair
We look for a sign that there's somebody there.

> But no one knows our pain
> No sympathy, no gain,
> And here we come, here we come
> Out of the darkness
> Again.

Out of the shadows and out of the shade,
Out of the miserable life we have made,
Glaring the sun down, and daring eclipse,
Hoping mortality offers its lips.

> Hoping someone knows our pain
> And with sympathy comes gain,
> So here we come, here we run
> Out of the darkness
> Again.

PAY THE PIPER

So you say you wanna dance all night,
Dark to light,
You wanna shake your soul,
Find a friend, pay a toll.
So you say you wanna dance all night,
Take a bite
Of life's bitter fruit,
Whatever will suit.
If the music enchants you, enhances your mind,
Fine.
I'll play along, I'll sing the song,
Then you can dance all night, all night long.

So you say you wanna dance all night,
Mind in flight,
Soar above the room,
The dark, the gloom.
So you say you wanna dance all night,
Fly not fight,
Keep above the fire,
Fly high then higher.
If the music enchants you, enhances your mind,
Fine.
I'll play along, I'll sing the song,
Then you can dance all night, all night long.

So you say you wanna dance all night,
Make wrong right,
Win the faerie prince,

Make the dragon mince,
So you say you wanna dance all night,
Ogres smite,
You wanna wave the wand,
Time and troubles gone.
If the music enchants you, enhances your mind,
Fine.
I'll play along, I'll sing the song,
Then you can dance all night, all night long.

But when daylight comes at last,
You'd better pay the piper fast
Or all you've wished the whole night through
Will turn and take a bite of you!
<spoken: PAY THE PIPER!>

RATTER
Ratter, ratter, mad as a hatter
I'll trap you, I'll zap you,
I'll slap you in the hall,
And it won't matter,
No, it won't matter,
No, it won't matter at all.

Hands down, or I'll swallow you whole,
Hands up, you gotta do as you're told . . .
Give me money or I'll take your soul,
Ratter!

Make a ring, or make yourself sing,
Make yourself a bodach or a fairy king,
I'll make you do any g-d thing,
Ratter!

Dance all morning, dance all night,
Dance into darkness or into the light,
You can never beat me in a fair fight,
Ratter!

Ratter, ratter, mad as a hatter
I'll trap you, I'll zap you,
I'll slap you in the hall,
And it won't matter,
No, it won't matter,
No, it won't matter at all.

GREEN IN THE BOWER
Green in the haven,
Green in the bower,
Green in the wide wold world all over.
The loveliest color that ever is seen.
In haven, in bower, is green green green.

Green is the heaven,
Green is the flower,
Green in the music the wide world over.
The loveliest color that ever is seen,
Is heaven, is power, is green green green.

Green in the grass tops,
Green in the fern,
Green in the growing,
The aching, the yearn,
Green in the leaf tips,
Green in the lawn,
Everyone's green
Till the moment they're gone.

Green is the hymning
Green is the power
Green is the living the wide world over.
Green is forgiving, for glamour, for seem,
The loveliest color is green green green green.

EXILE

Time and place mean nothing if you can't call them home.
Born of man and woman, you do not walk alone.
Me, I stalk the darkness, each solitary mile
Apart but not far distant—Exile.

Life and love mean little if you can't find a mate,
Immortality is but another word for fate.
I've never had a woman and I've never had a child,
Apart but not far distant—Exile.

Far off the rushing river sends out its serpent call,
The purple hills of Faerie, I still dream of them all.

When will I smell the heather, or again hear Faerie song?
I've nowhere now to love and I have nowhere I belong.

Time and place mean nothing if you have a fear of death.
Think too much of living and you cannot take a breath.
Think too much of weeping and you find you cannot smile,
Apart but not far distant—Exile.

GLAMOUR
I put the glamour on this space,
Transforming every human face,
And leaving nothing left to trace
When morning finally comes.

I put the magic on this spot
So what you see and think you've got,
And what you fear is what is not,
When morning finally comes.

> When morning comes
> The mundane morn
> When magic is
> No longer worn.

> When morning comes,
> The killer dawn
> When spells are done
> And magic gone

So stand upon my sacred ground
For what you hold's not what you've found,
And to this glamour you'll be bound
When morning finally comes.

STONE (NEVER RECORDED)
Unmoving, unchanging, a statue alone,
No wind nor weather, can alter the stone.
For stone cannot weep, and stone cannot feel,
Emotions are left to the mortal and real.